OWNED BY HER ENEMY

EVIE ROSE

Copyright © 2023 by Evie Rose

All rights reserved.

No part of this book may be reproduced in any form or by any electronic or mechanical means, including information storage and retrieval systems, without written permission from the author, except for the use of brief quotations in a book review.

This story is a work of fiction. Names, characters, places, and incidents are the product of the author's imagination or are used fictitiously. Any resemblance to actual events, locales, or persons, living or dead, is coincidental.

Cover: © 2023 by Evie Rose. Images under licence from Deposit Photos.

❦ Created with Vellum

CONTENT NOTES

These content notes are made available so readers can inform themselves if they want to. They're based on movie classification notes. Some readers might consider these as 'spoilers'.

- Bad language: frequent
- Sex: fully described sex scenes with dirty talk
- Violence: on and off page
- Other: death of parent, dubious consent, bondage, knife play, age gap, breeding, emotional abuse and captivity (in the past, but discussed on page),

1

LOTTE

The last time I left my father's gold tower in London was over three years ago for my mother's funeral. This time, it's to an exclusive restaurant to meet with the new head of the Edmonton bratva mafia: Nikolai Edmonton.

If we had peace with our oldest rivals, I think I could persuade my father to let me go out. I'd have videos of real outdoor settings instead of the shimmering, filled backgrounds. I'd have a chance to sneak away. I'd be free.

And that's why I talked my father into this meeting, and allowing me to join him. The restaurant we arrive at is in Lambeth territory, right in the centre of London. It's been redecorated recently, and treads the fine line between old-world character and modern.

Nikolai is already sitting at a long table in a private dining room, an untouched glass of red wine at his fingertips.

"Bastard," my father mutters. "He got here first. Now we look like the supplicants."

Which we are. We have to stop Edmonton bleeding us

dry, or the whole of Tottenham is going to crumble under its own weight.

He's compelling, the new bratva kingpin. Nikolai Edmonton is what you'd find in a Wikipedia picture under the listing, *London Mafia Bosses*. He's stone. Glistening, black stone. He has black hair with a slight curl, and short stubble shadowing his jawline, like we weren't even worth the credit of him shaving.

His grey eyes, though, really are stone. Marble perhaps. In those eyes there are a thousand hues, and none. They're mottled and the black pupils shine.

Power suits him. He's slipped into the role of leader like it was as made for him as I'm certain that suit was. He's been the head of the Edmonton Bratva for all of a month, and already established himself as brutal. Merciless.

First his uncle died. Then his brother's death was reported as "accidental", but there are rumours it was us, even though Nikolai benefitted. After that it got out that Nikolai executed five more of his family, and his lack of moral code was revealed. You don't kill *family*.

Yet something nudged at me to attempt this meeting. Perhaps it was just the success of my latest video, and the comment of my fan from the start, ListeningToHer, that this was my moment. ListeningToHer really believes in me, in a way that frankly I have given up on myself.

Nikolai skirts his gaze over my face with disinterest as my father and I sit.

Neither of them says anything, and despite the hubbub of chatter from the main restaurant leaking in through the walls into this private dining room, the tension is so thick it's like we're in soup. A waiter brings menus and we read in silence. He takes our orders and still there's a hush.

Nikolai is playing a power game, waiting for us to offer the first greeting. But my father won't. Knowing he's in a weaker position makes him petty. *We* must have peace between our families though. If I could just get out a few times, I could find a way to escape. That means Edmonton and Tottenham must give up this stupid feud, so my father won't have the excuse to keep me locked up any longer.

The waiting staff serves our starters, and my father pauses. For a second, I think no one will eat for fear of being poisoned. Then Nikolai takes one of his oysters in the shell, brings it to his lips, and slides the whole little bite into his mouth.

Those lips. Plush and wide and with a sinful tilt. He licks them as he finishes chewing and the satisfied look on his face would infuriate me if I could stop watching his neck. Mostly covered by his crisp white shirt, the black stubble and the hard lump of his Adam's apple is compelling. I squeeze my thighs together under the table as my pussy heats.

Why does he have to be so gorgeous? Yeah, he's my dad's age, but that's where the similarities end. David Tottenham has a blond combover he thinks no one has noticed, a poorly fitted suit, and a paunch.

I take after my mother. A pang of grief goes through me, familiar in its pain. Dark hair, dark brown eyes, skin that tans easily if I'm out in the sun.

Though being outside at all is rare for me now.

Nikolai reaches for another oyster, and I jerk my gaze to the goat cheese and asparagus salad before me. I can't bear this.

"My condolences on your brother and father." I didn't even realise I was going to break the silence until I did. I gulp down a mouthful of wine, and surely, it's the alcohol that warms me as our enemy directs his attention to my face.

Nikolai tilts his chin up and narrows his eyes.

"My condolences for the loss of your mother. She went the same way as my brother, I understand."

There's a beat when I can't breathe. My chest seizes up and I seriously think I might die too. Because is he confessing what I think he is?

The arrogant expression on his face suggests, yes. I'm not misreading.

My father has told me time and time again that the reason I can't leave the tower is because it's too dangerous. That the bratva killed my mother, and Antonio her bodyguard, in a car bomb. We didn't even have a body to bury.

And for three years, I've had my doubts. There's no love between me and my father. But here this bratva bastard kingpin is, making it clear the cause is the same. The feud killed his brother and my mother.

"You dare offer sympathy," my father growls. "When you..."

Edmonton raises one eyebrow, and my father trails off into resentful silence.

"When I *what?*" the bratva kingpin mocks. "You murdered both my parents, then have the gall to—"

"Your family has suffered greatly from this feud recently." My father launches into what sounds like a pre-prepared speech. "Since you are new to this role, I came to talk about increasing our mutual profitability and sustainability by negotiating peace terms between our families."

"Why should I? You're losing this war. I'll destroy you soon enough." His voice is iron.

My father grits his teeth. "What's the price of peace, Edmonton?"

"Your daughter."

Shock reverberates through the room. The new kingpin doesn't even look my way, despite having allowed me a seat at the table. He lounges back in his chair, a dangerous big cat toying with his prey.

"My daughter is not an object to be given away," my father blusters.

"And yet you keep her locked up in your tower, your caged bird. There's stolen art that leaves London more often than she does."

Neither of them have actually said my name.

My heart hammers. This isn't what I had in mind. I might finally escape Tottenham Tower, but I can see a new prison, ready for me to be shoved through the door and left to rot. Or simply murdered as retribution because Nikolai is as alone as I am. Tottenham disappeared most of his family, even if he did some of our job for us.

I'm just a little white mouse to this man. He'll kill me as soon as he tires of the game. Maybe as a point.

Shit.

"You took my wife, and now you want my only daughter?" My father's gaze darts to me and there's the familiar distaste on his face. He's not asking what Edmonton intends to do with me, merely posturing. I'm a pretty doll that my father protects. I'm a walking Ming vase.

An ugly snarl draws up Nikolai's mouth, contempt in every line. "You don't have anything else to offer, do you?" he taunts. "You're broke. In debt up to your double chins."

How does he know that?

"I know a great deal about Tottenham that I'm sure you

do not want public," he adds, as though he read my mind. Or maybe the distress on my face. "This feud can only be ended by a symbol. A marriage."

Married. To him? This monster who stole my mother from me now wants to take my chance at liberty?

No. No way.

This is not going how I'd hoped.

I thought there would be more... offers? Discussion? At least the main course of dinner. More something. *Opportunities.*

"If you want to keep your secrets, I suggest you agree to my exceedingly reasonable demands."

I expect my father to protest, but he pushes coleslaw ineffectually on his plate.

The thought of eating roils my stomach. But Nikolai has no such qualms. He calmly tips another oyster into his mouth, smirking.

"Delicious," he murmurs.

This arrogant kingpin will own me before long, I realise. All my plans of escape will be shards of porcelain on the floor if I'm not able to find an alternative price for peace that Nikolai will accept, and my father will agree to.

My father will cave. I steal a glance at him. Yeah. He's wondering if he can get away with such a cheap price as the daughter he only keeps as a status symbol because I'm beautiful and can sing at the events he hosts for his cronies.

A new cage, this one with my mother's killer.

And suddenly, I see the way out. I wouldn't murder my father—whatever he's done, I'm first and foremost a Tottenham. My heritage is crucial. Knowing where I came from, who my family is. That was what my mother told me, again and again. Family is everything.

But my enemy? The one who is responsible, even if indirectly, for my mother's death?

Yeah. I'd kill him in a heartbeat. And as his wife, I'd have the access I'd need to do it. A wedding night. I still have my V-card, but if I'm tarnishing my soul, what's giving up my innocence?

I look at Nikolai afresh. Will he fall for it? Might he want to slake his lust on his sheltered little virgin wife?

He licks his fingers clean as he finishes his last oyster, and something springs in my tummy as our eyes meet. Yeah. I think he could be tempted. He's a man. They're all beasts at their core, right? I'll wear white, act sweet, and he won't be able to resist rutting me.

And then I'll stab him in that gorgeous neck of his. Let *him* bleed virgin blood all over the bed covers.

Revenge and freedom.

It isn't what I'd imagined, but I'm thrilled. It's better.

"Father." I cast my eyes demurely down. Ha. What a lie. "I know you're hesitating because you believe you can't ask this of me."

"Charlotte—"

"It's okay. I understand my duty as your daughter. My loyalty is to Tottenham, but if you think this is best, I will submit."

Nikolai has wry amusement and proud satisfaction playing around his mouth when I flick my eyes up to his face.

"Your honour is besmirched by this bad deal," my father growls out, but I note he doesn't say no. He's talking about it as though it's already done.

"I'll take her today."

My father splutters.

"Now," Nikolai clarifies. This man loves to be in charge,

in authority. I'm amazed he managed under the old kingpin and then his brother for so long. Except, I suppose he didn't. His brother was kingpin for only a month.

"You disgusting heathen, you think I'll let my daughter go with you immediately?"

A swell of surprised comfort rises in my chest. He cares about me, after all?

"If we're having an arranged marriage to cement the peace deal between our families, it will be in public, with a big wedding. Not in this grubby backroom."

The warmth recedes. Yeah, back to being a precious vase. He wants to ensure this fully benefits him.

The urge to check notifications on my phone nearly overwhelms me. I want to talk to ListeningToHer. I probably would if I had any pockets for said phone in this slinky red silk dress.

Whenever I'm lonely I sing. And in the last year, I open social media, record myself singing with the sea or a mountain trail in the background, and upload it to an account no one knows about. Then I'm just Rapunzel, the girl with a soulful voice and fans who love it when I sing about finding love.

It's fiction. A dream far from my reality. But when I see dots bouncing and the name ListeningToHer, I get this weird sense of peace. They were my first follower and always write the first comment, praising my voice, how brave I am, my song choice, my smile. And when we go back and forth with messages, I'm both less alone and more free.

Which, for a girl trapped in a tower by a mafia war, is a pretty big deal.

"Three weeks." Nikolai taps his fingers on the table. "Organise the biggest wedding London has seen in two lifetimes. Make the Royal wedding look modest. My fiancée will plan it all, but nothing is done at Tottenham Towers. She goes to every bridal shop, every caterer, every venue. With me."

"Absolutely not." My father sounds outraged. "I haven't protected her all these years to allow you to steal her before the deal is done under the guise of wedding tasks."

"And I will pay."

"So generous," my father sneers. "You just don't want to admit the only way you can get a bride is by extortion."

"Indeed." Nikolai smiles bitterly. "Your daughter is the only one for me."

I seriously doubt that. A man as beautiful—and powerful—as Nikolai Edmonton could have any woman in London. He's picked me because... Why? He's close to destroying the Tottenham mafia altogether. But then, there has been a lot of blood split recently. He'll know that Tottenham won't go down without taking a chunk of his Bratva flesh with it. And he's right. The only thing of value Tottenham has now is me.

"Not *with you*." My father's lips are in a line thin enough to be the legal veneer of Tottenham's businesses.

Nikolai shrugs. "Three of my men and whatever lap dogs you employ accompany her, but my fiancée goes in person to make every arrangement."

"If you really need an unpaid lackey to plan a wedding, we can accommodate you." My father continues eating, a snooty expression on his face.

The Bratva kingpin reaches into his inner suit jacket pocket and tosses a matte black credit card onto the table before me. "Any questions?"

With shaking hands, I draw the card to me. It's in my name.

Yes. Yes, I have a million questions. Firstly, I can't

believe it. I'm going to leave Tottenham Tower. Something expands in my chest. Excitement maybe? With at least six guards, since there's no way my father will allow Edmonton men to outnumber Tottenham, so zero chance of escape. But still. I'll breathe fresh air.

"Your unreasonable demands are very clear," my father huffs.

"Good. You may go," Nikolai says dismissively. "Unless you're going to leave her as dessert."

Nikolai smirks as my father goes the colour beetroot. Speechless. Impotent. This bratva bastard has all the cards in this game, and we all know it.

But when we're in bed, and his guard is down, I'll have a knife.

"Three weeks. You better be there, Edmonton," my father throws down his cutlery and storms out, chair banging to the floor.

I scurry to follow, but I can't resist one glance backwards.

My fiancé flashes a smile at me, a bit crooked. A lot devilish. He's far too attractive for his own good.

Hope he enjoys it, because he won't be so pretty when he's dead.

I turn and try to flee, but at the door, I hear his voice, soft as if only for me.

"Until our wedding day, Rapunzel."

The floor drops away. My head snaps back to look at him. He's smiling. So smug. Arrogant.

I stagger from the room in a daze.

"What did he say?" my father hisses when I catch up with him, propelling me forwards with a hand between my shoulder blades.

"You're a puzzle," I lie instinctively.

Because the Bratva kingpin knows.

He knows about my singing. About my secret account. He knew about the Tottenham finances, and I can't help but fear what else he might know…

He's my enemy. And I think he knows everything.

2

NIKOLAI

What I should be doing: triple checking the security at the wedding venue, glowering at my fellow mafia bosses to keep them in line, reminding my Edmonton relatives this is my decision and they can keep their opinions about the Tottenhams to themselves, acting cool and like I don't care that I'm waiting for my bride at the biggest mafia wedding London has seen since the Westminster kingpin got married to his son's ex-girlfriend, chastising myself for being a twisted bastard forcing a girl half my age to marry me.

What I'm actually doing: watching Rapunzel's old videos with the sound off as I stand at the front of the church, waiting for the new one I know she'll post soon.

The priest has coughed four times, trying to hint to me that it's not polite to ignore my guests or focus on my phone while in a crumbling stack of so-called holy stones. Mikhail, my second-in-command is doing his best to look calm. The Tottenhams are restless, casting dark looks at the Edmontons.

Honestly, I don't give a fuck about any of that.

My only interest is my fiancée.

Rapunzel.

It started innocently enough, for the mafia. My first job for Edmonton was as a digital spy, proving my worth by infiltrating Tottenham over twenty-five years ago, when I was just a kid. I was the one keeping track of information going in and out when we were still using CDs and analogue.

More recently it's all very dull. The internet makes things simple. Bankrupting a greedy pig like Tottenham is not as difficult as it sounds when you have as much access to his online world as I do. Watching everything that went on in Tottenham and silently scuppering each attempt David Tottenham made was savagely satisfying. I was in a digital tower, a lone, all-powerful man making slights of hand—the occasional email lost, a "typo" or two that changed the whole meaning. Every step that inexorably progressed to disaster was seemingly an accident.

The opening of a social media account was of only marginal interest to me. I'd watched Charlotte Tottenham thousands of times as she grew up, but never felt anything. At forty, I prefer experience and brevity in my bed partners, not youth. If they're going to cry, I want it to be because that's their kink and I have my hand around their throat, not because their little virgin cunt can't take my big cock.

I played the video to observe and scheme, not to fall in love.

She'd called herself Rapunzel, which made me curious: the girl imprisoned in a tower. That name hinted Charlotte Tottenham was not the spoiled mafia princess I'd assumed.

From the first note, I swear my soul left my body and has been floating around, searching for her, since. She wore the same red dress as I saw her in at our restaurant first meeting, and had a filter that made her hair smooth and her face cartoony. But it was the tone of her voice that ripped me apart. So sweet and mournful, singing about lost love.

I did something out of character for me: I left a comment on the video, saying she had the most amazing talent. Then another compliment on the next one, and the next. A year later and we're conversing every day.

In those messages we're friends. In reality, she's the daughter of my sworn enemy.

"Boss, her car has stopped a couple of streets away." Mikhail sounds tense.

I nod to reassure him. He hasn't understood that I'm not actually as psychotic and bloodthirsty as the reputation I've built. Quite the opposite.

It was simple. My uncle planned to blow up the whole Tottenham Tower—prick thought he could blame brown people and get away with it. But anything that risked harming my girl? Not going to happen.

He died of a very plausible heart attack. When my brother voiced his intention to continue with the same plan, he died in a tragically preventable drug overdose.

But I'd learned by that point. To protect my girl, I had to be the kingpin. I took over, called the entire Edmonton Bratva family together and forced them all to give up their phones so I could control the narrative. Then I asked who wanted to go ahead with the attack on Tottenham Tower and shot every last one who raised their hand.

Not so much "touch her and die", more "even think of touching her and die".

The story I put out was that they challenged my authority. I prefer to be more subtle, as I was with my brother and uncle, I leave a body and a clear reason for the death. I'm never cruel to those left behind. I know the pain of being denied closure since Tottenham murdered my parents. They just disappeared, as is Tottenham's sadistic hallmark.

After that, a suggestion here and there, a bit more financial pressure, and David Tottenham invited me to discuss peace. Childishly easy.

"Boss, think of how it looks—"

"She'll be here," I cut Mikhail off.

He's quick, and loyal, but prone to telling me things I already know. Not his fault.

Lotte has stopped to make what she fears will be her last video as Rapunzel. Usually she does a few takes, and I enjoy watching those far more than is healthy. This time though...

She looks into the camera, her glossy dark brown hair falling over her eyes. The background is a long sandy beach with a bright blue sky. When she moves, a tone of black follows her.

She sings a hauntingly beautiful aria. It's fancy. Maybe in Italian? I've got it on my phone speaker playing in full sight, in a damn church. Out of the corner of my eye, Mikhail looks like he might be sick, and in the front row of pews Grant Lambeth exchanges a confused look with his wife. Fucker. I'd tell him and his opinions to get out if I cared about anyone but Lotte.

As she tails off the high note, she smiles wryly into the camera, and says, "Just wanted to let you know that I'll be away for a bit. Bye for now."

And that's it.

I type in a message, as she'll be expecting. I'm vaguely aware that the entire church is watching me text my fiancée after I played her singing to the hushed room.

> ListeningToHer: Gorgeous. But everything okay, songbird?

> Rapunzel: TBH, I don't know.

Oof. Her honesty kills me sometimes. She has no idea that I'll take care of her in every way.

> Rapunzel: Just think I'll be limited in what I can post.

My ptichka has obviously heard about how I don't allow my team to keep any technology that might compromise us. To be fair, we've binned a lot of phones and she's right. I won't risk her continuing to use her current one.

> ListeningToHer: You'll still sing, I hope.

> Rapunzel: Maybe. Does that even matter if you can't hear it? Like that thing about a tree falling in a wood and nobody hearing, does it actually fall?

> ListeningToHer: Your singing matters if it makes you happy.

> Rapunzel: Not exactly.

> ListeningToHer: Matters to me. And your happiness.

> Rapunzel: Thank you. Ditto. <3

She does that sometimes and I note she doesn't send casual hearts to anyone else. I try not to read too much into it, because I know that it will be a hard fight to get her to accept me as her husband in truth.

But maybe it'll be enough to protect her, make her

happy, and gradually earn her trust, little though I deserve it.

> ListeningToHer: See you soon.

> Rapunzel: I wish.

And that makes me smile as I slide my phone into my pocket. I focus on the entrance of the church. She'll be here.

My heart bubbles over when she appears in the doorway. My girl is here to marry me. Really here. I take her in, lingering over her face that is partially obscured by a delicate white veil, so her expression is a mystery. The curves of her body, though... That dress. Hell, I don't know what it cost. Half Edmonton's fortune for all I care because the white silk and lace fit her perfectly. She's gorgeous in anything, but in a dress *she* chose to marry *me*, that *I* paid for?

Perfection.

Music swells, and I can't tell whether that's in my head or reality until the whole church stands.

She's graceful as a swan gliding down the aisle towards me and the vision is marred by two things. Not being able to see her face, and her sneering father at her elbow.

David Tottenham doesn't even attempt to hide his disgust as he places Lotte's hand in mine. In response, I don't try to keep in the self-satisfied smile that tugs at my lips.

I've won. She's going to be mine. First my wife, then my lover. My sweetheart. My soul.

She has her head tilted down, and she's shorter than me, so with the veil her thoughts are entirely blocked off.

I take her hand and draw her to my side. "Good of you to turn up, ptichka."

"It is, isn't it." She tilts her chin up and I have the disconcerting feeling that she can see me, but I can't see her. It's foreign, and I don't like it. Normally I'm the one shrouded in darkness, seeing her but hidden myself.

"You look lovely. What is visible, that is." The veil is impeding my view and my fingers itch to rip it off.

"Thank you," she says, then adds under her breath, "for the obligatory compliment on the only thing about a woman worthy of a man's notice. Let's get this over with."

I hold back a laugh. She's not going to make this easy, but I'm ready for that.

Straightening her shoulders, and standing to her full height of practically a dwarf, she faces the front of the church.

I nod to the priest, and he begins. The ceremony is fucking long enough for me to grow an inch of beard and impatient. It's a supreme effort not to grab Lotte, throw her over my shoulder, and steal her away. But she did her job well; we'll be here until midnight with food and drink, fireworks, and music. It will be hours and hours until it's just the two of us.

I snatch her wedding ring from Mikhail when that moment arrives, but hesitate when I find I have a ring as well as her. I thought... The idea of wearing her ring ripples through me. A sign of her ownership of me, and she chose it. So although none of these stupid formal phrases mean anything, and this whole event is a farce to get her tied to me, my heart jumps to my throat when I take her hand in mine and slip the platinum band over her finger. I have to choke out the words about "with this ring" and whatever bullshit because I'm fixated on the matching ring Mikhail has waiting.

Her expression is screened, and her tone is even, neutral, as she repeats the same phrases and slides the gold onto my finger. And hell, she probably just bought it because it enabled her to spend more time away from Tottenham Tower, but I've never worn a piece of jewellery in my life, and it's heavy. A link between her and me.

The rest of the ceremony goes by in a blur, until, "You may kiss the bride."

That's it. We're married. There's a collective sigh of relief from behind us as everyone who isn't a Tottenham or Edmonton relaxes.

Slowly, I reach out with both hands and grip the flimsy edge of the veil, pulling it up, revealing her face. For a second defiance fires in her expression. Anger, pure and hot. Then it's swiftly covered over with sweet innocence.

Interesting.

I cup her jaw gently in my palm and lower my head to hers. Our kiss is light. A brush of lips.

She draws away with a gasp, and that triggers something in me. I grab her. Crush her to me, and the beast inside me roars. I hold her, my hand a necklace, my thumb over her throat. My kiss this time is brutal, a savage thing that possesses me and claims her. I kiss her like she's air, as though I could eat her up. There are murmurs around us of polite concern. She makes a muffled squeak and for a second her lips part, soft and accepting, her hand on my shoulder pulling me closer.

Then she shoves, and I release her.

"That's enough!" she hisses, staring up at me like a disgruntled mouse yelling at an elephant.

Is it?

No. It's not enough. It'll never be enough until she is wild with lust and love and begging me to take her. Until she's mine in every way.

But she's right, it's enough for now. And I don't mind keeping up the facade of a reluctant bridegroom. It wouldn't do for Tottenham to know how entirely I've won this battle.

I give a mocking bow and offer my hand. Applause breaks out as we walk down the aisle to the orchestral version of the first song she ever posted. I wonder if she recognises it?

At the door, we pause as the photographers catch up, snapping from all sides.

My palm on her waist, keeping her close, I lean down.

"Just wait until I get you home," I growl into her ear. "With all the fluff you've arranged it'll be late, but it's not *enough* until I say it is." There are many things I want to show my *wife*.

3

LOTTE

I planned it this way, but our wedding day is gruelling. A marathon of eating, dancing, clapping, watching. There is a week's worth of entertainment. My new husband doesn't leave my side during any of it.

The wedding ring is unnatural on my finger. Heavy. It's one link of a chain that weighs me down as my ill-fated husband helps me from the limo outside his house. Unlike Tottenham Tower, Edmonton's house isn't open to the street, instead having a short but sweeping driveway, hidden in trees, that leads to the front steps. The glimpse I have of the building is an impression of an imposing, traditional design, with sash windows and stones in lines rather than modern glass and steel.

Edmonton is as refined as Tottenham is brash.

"I'll show you your rooms," Nikolai says as he leads me up a sculpted grand wooden staircase, all dark floral wallpaper and plush carpets that soften our footsteps. "My bedroom is there if you need anything." He indicates a door then walks in the opposite direction. "I suggest you sleep, and we talk in the morning. It's been a long day."

He shows me sitting rooms that are all understated luxury. No chrome and hard lines here. It's all quality and elegance. Different though this house may be, as I follow him down a corridor to yet another sitting room for my use, my skin is too small. I have to get out of here.

So, when we finally get to a bedroom, I halt abruptly.

"Aren't we going to consummate our marriage?" I blurt out, and he stops walking halfway to another door, and yet another room.

I think in bed, as he's in the throes of pleasure, his guard down, would be the perfect time to kill him. I try not to think about why I'm circling back around to that idea, rather than just knifing him in the back in the kitchen while he's eating breakfast. Less dramatic, sure, but usually I'm a practical kind of person. It's almost like I kind of want him to take my virginity.

It's not that. Obviously.

Much.

"Do you want us to have sex?" he asks as he turns, then looks me up and down dispassionately.

I can't say no, because that's not true. I do want him, almost as much as I want to kill him. But yes isn't an option either, because I don't want to seem eager. That'll tip him off.

"I'll do my duty."

He barks out a laugh. "No, that's not enough."

"It's an arranged marriage," I say with a huff. "What do you expect?"

"I expect you to beg me," he replies softly, his voice deep and resonating through me like the bass of a favourite song. "I expect you to be desperate for my cock. I want your pussy creaming and so wet you're dripping with need. You'll be shaking with desire when I take you."

Oh. My jaw is slack. Despite the fact that isn't going to happen and is antithetical to my aims, the way he says it, in a low rumble that liquifies my belly, draws me in.

"And we're not there yet, are we?" He doesn't expect a reply, it seems as he slides his hands into his pockets and strolls away. "There's one more room I want to show you, ptichka."

He's called me that a few times, and I'm tempted to ask what the Russian accented word means. I restrain my curiosity and follow.

Let's get this over with.

He opens the door wide and gestures for me to enter with a hint of a secret smile around his mouth, like he's looking forward to my response when I've been politely positive about everything thus far.

I need him to trust me, or at least want me, so I try to be curious and happy. I really do, as I look into the room. It's small.

My back seizes up at how small.

He's not your father. He might be a monster, but he will be different.

I step inside. The walls are covered with foam, and my chest tightens. Then I see the microphone. The recording equipment.

It's a recording studio. Nothing bad about this. Nothing at all.

I can't breathe.

"I heard you like to sing," he says from behind me. "Thought you might want to try recording yourself with more than just your phone."

"Is this sound proofing so no one can hear your bride scream?" I cover the prickle of fear with a joke. Probably a joke.

But this man is the bratva. The bogeyman.

"When I make you scream, neither of us will care who hears." And though it's said in a silky tone, I'm not sure if it's a threat or... Something else. And it's not exactly scary, but my mind repeats different words with the same calm tone in a tiny room.

The walls aren't moving. They're not, but I'm breathing too fast. My vision blurs.

Oh shit oh shit oh shit.

Nikolai is speaking to me, but I can't hear over the rush of blood in my ears. All I can see is my room in Tottenham Tower. The gold door handle and the white walls. The quiet and the glass that doesn't move. The tiny bathroom and the unending silence. The boredom. Loneliness and lack of touch. Same walls day after day, same food, day after day. The silence. Trying the handle and the door not moving. Never moving.

The walls shift around me. I'm stumbling. I grab for the door. There isn't enough air in this room, and I throw myself out, chest heaving. My head flops forward and while some rational part of my brain knows I'm not in Tottenham Tower, Nikolai isn't my father, and I have a plan to escape this whole mafia trap, my body hasn't understood.

A thought crackles through my mind: is this a panic attack?

"Ptichka?" A warm hand rests on my shoulder blade, and that cuts through—a little. I'm acting like a crazy woman.

"I need..." I have to get out I can't breathe I can't breathe. "*Air.*"

"Here."

There's a blast of cool air and I gasp it in. Then I'm being propelled outside—*outside!*—into the cool night. I drag in lungfuls of air, palms holding onto something solid and comforting. My cheek rests on soft cotton.

A few ragged breaths, then a few more. As my eyes focus, I find the dark glow of the London skyline, familiar and faraway, and below, trees. A garden. Sweeping arcs of flower bushes and smooth grass. A seat under a rose arch and a deep border of flowers that even in the dark I can see is a cascade of colour. And a perfectly round pool with a fountain in the middle.

It's beautiful. An oasis in the middle of London.

I'm on a balcony, I realise. Unlike Tottenham Tower, with its hermetically sealed thick glass, this house has windows and outside space, even on the upper floors.

As my desperation for oxygen recedes, going back to the normal, unthinking process, I take in what else is going on. I'm pressed to Nikolai's chest, clinging to his lapels. And my next breath brings in his scent. Fresh as the night, but with warm spice too.

"I'm sorry. Rapunzel wasn't just a name, was it?" He's murmuring softly and running his hands over my arms and shoulders, soothing me like I'm a wild animal. "My ptichka. I should have known."

These words make no sense to me, but I can't help but give a shuddering sigh and keep holding onto him like I'd be sucked back into the house if I let him go.

"I would have taken you to Cornwall tonight if I'd realised."

His hand slips up and strokes my hair, and I nearly purr at how good it is to be held. It's been a long, long time.

"I didn't think... I'd have got you out sooner if I had," he murmurs.

Perhaps it's the cold finally biting into my skin, or Nikolai echoing what my heart longed for over the years since my mother's death—for someone to rescue me and they never did—but I'm alert.

I survived being locked in my bedroom for months at a time. I've left Tottenham Tower.

And I'm *nearly out*.

One more action, and then freedom. Never having to be trapped ever again. I'll find my friends who watch my videos and tell ListeningToHer how they kept me afloat, and I'll sing whenever I want. Yes, this will be a bloody step I've never made before, but what's the alternative? Being another man's captive.

No way.

I'm suddenly aware of the razor blade hidden in the underwire of my bra, and why I carefully wrapped tape over and secured it. To kill Nikolai Edmonton, and run away.

If I could elicit a kiss, maybe we'd end up having sex? He's holding me, isn't he? That has to mean something. I turn a little and tilt my head up, looking into his eyes. They seemed like stone earlier, but his irises are silver in the moonlight.

Parting my lips, it's not difficult to fake passion and gratitude. My heart beats with it as I whisper, "Kiss me."

For a second, I'm sure he will, but he shakes his head, once. From one side to the other and my stomach sinks. Just a short denial.

"That recording booth wasn't what you wanted," he states, looking down into my face. "I'm sorry."

"It doesn't matter now." A single hug can't change that he killed my mother, and I lick my lips. His gaze dips to look and I swear desire flares between us.

"What do you want most in the world?" He puts me away from him. Not fast, and with reluctance that seems like he's moving through honey, but firmly, until I'm no longer in his arms and the chilled air nips at all the places we touched.

To kill you and have my freedom.

I shrug. "To go and sing somewhere with a real background. The beach, or something." I've longed to be by the sea.

"Tomorrow." He nods. "We'll do that tomorrow."

And then he's gone, leaving me on the balcony, staring at the night sky, confused.

4

LOTTE

I hesitate at my new husband's bedroom door. An hour ago, he left me without so much as a goodnight.

But I can't stop thinking about the look in his eyes and, disastrous as it was, how a recording studio of my own is a gesture that speaks of some thought having gone into our marriage. If I allow this to go on for too long, I'll end up romanticising what is undoubtedly manipulation by a powerful man.

It's a mouse knock on his door, scared of my own boldness. Terrified by my fear and my intentions.

"Come."

Nikolai is sprawled on a leather sofa, a tatty paperback in one hand and a glass of amber liquid in the other.

"What if I *wanted* us to consummate our marriage?"

He quirks an eyebrow as he looks up. "Ready to beg, ptichka? I thought you had more pride."

"We're married." I square my shoulders, then internally wince. That's really not the seduction vibes I was thinking of. "I'm a virgin. This might only be an arranged marriage, but I have my pride, and so do you. If it gets out that I'm still an innocent, it'll jeopardise the deal."

Setting down his book, he takes a sip of whisky and palms down the front of his trousers. And oh shit. There's an intimidating bulge there. He's hard. And huge. My mouth waters and something in my tummy does a flip.

His expression remains neutral. "Are you wet for me?"

I... he's so crass, and yet. Yeah. I like it. I enjoy the way his gaze lingers on the swell of my breasts. I had to transfer the blade into the waistband of the little white silk pyjamas I'm wearing, but the press of that cool metal is nothing compared to the flame of desire that twists up my insides.

"Between your legs. Are you squirming with the thought of me inside you? Are you needy?"

"Yes." And while not exactly true, it's definitely not a lie. I am getting more and more turned on by him as we speak. There's something about his presence. He's much bigger than me, and when he cradled me in his arms as I had a meltdown over a small room, he didn't even force me or lock me into, I felt safe. Cherished.

"Take off your clothes, come here, and show me your pussy is soaking," he commands, and I freeze.

He's calling my bluff.

If I remove my clothes, how will I murder him? Never mind, never mind. I'm earning his trust. Lulling him into a false sense of security. Maybe I'll kill him in his sleep.

But my hands shake as I bring them to the little silk top I changed into. The last thing I see as I pull it over my head is his eyes going dark. It's vulnerable as the silk brushes over my face. Then it's over, it's off and I blink at the light as I tug my hair free. Although my bare tits are just there, nipples pert—and this is what he wanted, right? He asked for me to get naked—he's watching my eyes.

I take a step towards him, but he clatters the glass of whisky onto a table and holds up a hand to stop me approaching further.

"Now the rest."

Hell, I thought men were supposed to lose their minds and become animals the moment they saw exposed flesh? But Nikolai is in no danger of losing control as I slide the pyjama shorts down my thighs.

Then the silk is pooled at my feet and my cheeks are heating as Nikolai still doesn't look at my body, remaining apparently relaxed, one big hand cupped over the bulge of his erection, and the other carelessly laid on the arm of the sofa.

He nods and I take that as a signal to approach, leaving my pyjamas and means of killing him on the carpet behind me. I hesitate as I step closer, my heart pounding. Languidly, he eases forward and clasps my thighs, guiding me to stand between his knees. The brush of fabric and his warm palms on my naked skin makes me feel suddenly very exposed.

And my treacherous body likes it. Likes *him*, my husband I'm going to... My brain shies away from the thought as excitement bubbles through me. My pussy throbs. He's fully clothed, chin tilted up, eyes on my face, and I'm standing over him.

In this moment I'm powerful and wicked, and also at his mercy. It's a heady combination.

"Spread your legs for me."

There's no doubt this is supposed to be scary and humiliating, but I must be wired wrong, because it's hot as hell. As I step out until my knees brush his trousers I feel the moisture from my pussy, slick and sticky.

"That's it." He smiles slightly, just the merest upturn of

the corner of his mouth, as I'm motionless again, waiting for his instructions. With deliberate slowness, he smooths his hand across my thigh, until he lightly covers the gap between my legs. His silver eyes glitter as his fingers slide down, and cup my pussy. Then one finger brushes over my folds, and though it's a gentle touch, it flares excitement right to my core. My pussy clenches.

His finger glides through the slickness, and we both know what he's found, our gazes lock.

I'm wet for him.

"Excellent," he croons and it's like that single word sends pleasure pulsing down my spine. "You're a good girl for telling me the truth. I'm pleased with you."

It's a simple compliment, but my body's reaction to this reckless game we're playing is outrageous. It's heady. I want his praise on repeat in my ears all day. It's instantaneously my favourite ever song.

He withdraws his hand and brings it to his mouth, staring into my eyes as he inhales the scent of where the cream from between my legs has wetted his fingers. There's uncensored enjoyment in his expression and I sway on my feet. I'm rocked. He... Did he just...?

"But not wet enough, because I have a big cock and you're only little. I need you dripping when I take you."

I let out an involuntary mew that sounds an awful lot like disappointment.

"Don't worry, we can do other things." In one movement, he stands and sweeps me up. There's no warning before his strong arms are under my upper back and my knees, and I grasp at his chest for stability. That's not needed though, as he has me secure. He strides to the bed and throws me onto it.

I barely have time to shriek as I hit the mattress before

he drags me to the edge, kneels on the floor and tosses my thighs over his shoulders.

"You want me to take your virginity? First things first. Has a man ever licked you here?" He presses a kiss right onto my slit.

"No," I gasp out as I try to sit up and see what he's intending to do.

"Good," he snarls, and the next moment my clit is in his mouth. He's sucking it and I fall back against the covers, jerking at the intensity, a moan ripped from me.

I've touched myself down there, and thought I knew what I liked. But as it turns out, I had no clue. Because Nikolai is using more pressure than I'd ever apply, and it's amazing. Plus, the scruff of his jaw rubs against my skin and the contrast heightens the pleasure. I'm boneless, a creature who belongs to him, held by him. It's almost too much, and without my volition, I writhe away.

"Nope." His arm bands over my lower belly, pressing me down and keeping me exactly where he wants me. When his hand finds my breast, squeezing and pinching the nipple I cry out.

"You're going to take what I give you like a good girl."

He redoubles his efforts and I squirm, desperate for more and almost in pain from how wonderful it feels.

He's my enemy and this is a fight. A battle.

And I'm losing.

I can't remember what I came to his room for, because my head is entirely filled with *him*. His scent, his body, the things he's doing to me, his very presence. Most of all, the attention he's lavishing on my virgin pussy. There's no space for anything but the rising tide of tension in between my legs and sparks over my skin where he touches me.

Someone keens, a long high note that resonates in the

air, that's joined by a deep bass rumble of approval, and it's *us*.

His hand leaves my breast and strokes firmly down my body in what I recognise as being a possessive claim. A mapping of his territory all the way to my entrance, where he slips between my folds and pushes his fingers into me like he owns me. As though he has the right to do this, which I suppose as my husband, he does. There's no hesitation and he's still licking at my clit all this time.

Then he's stroking me from the inside out, surrounding me, invading every part.

The orgasm tears through me. It's a pitch that shatters glass and resonates through my body. I swear it changes me at a molecular level as my legs shake uncontrollably, the pleasure reaching down to my toes and, implausibly, up to my heart. It's heat and wrecking power, an earthquake, and a volcano. I have no brain, just a clenching pussy that holds onto his fingers like it would eat them if it could.

It's all I can do to clutch the sheets and dig my heels into his back, holding on as though I might be ripped out of this world.

As the pleasure recedes, I'm not sure my body will ever be the same again. That orgasm reduced parts of me to rubble that I thought were immoveable walls, high and strong. I'm so wiped out, I could fall asleep in this daze.

"So fucking pretty, my debauched girl."

My eyes drag open to find my husband standing over me. He's released his cock, but remains otherwise fully dressed. And that massive cock is in his fist, being pumped hard, almost violently. His mouth glistens with my juices, all the way to his cheeks. He gorged on me.

"Mine," he rumbles.

I thought I was utterly destroyed, and I am, and yet that

possessive word sends an aftershock through me. I'm compelled to look at him. Nothing binds me, and he's a virtual stranger, yet my blood sings through my veins and I remain motionless for him, as much his captive as if he'd pinned me down to the bed. His face is creased in a snarl, and he's focused entirely on me. Similarly, I can't take my eyes off him, my gaze flicking between his face and where his hand is driving up and down his cock. The head is red and angry, and down the length there's a thick vein. The sight of his cock makes my tired body ache for more. It's beautiful. Scary. Intimidating as a storm.

And mouth watering.

"Ptichka," he groans.

Hot liquid smacks me, and I gasp. His come. He's covering me with line after line of creamy white. They're stripes over my breasts, belly, and my mons and hit as sharp as a cut, like this is permanent. A tattoo.

It's primal. Dirty. The air is thick with the scent of my sex and his—and his is musky and so good I want to rub it into my skin. I raise my gaze back to his face.

He doesn't close his eyes as he shudders with his release, his expression savagely beautiful in the low light. It shakes me anew as a final hot stripe hits. I'd almost say he looks obsessed, if it weren't the first time we've ever interacted only two weeks ago.

"*My wife.*" His frantic movements ease.

He *owns* me.

The thought is too much, and I close my eyes against the blazing heat of this whole experience. Of him. I'm sticky and warm between my legs, and all over my breasts too. I'm used-up and sated and exhausted.

I'm his *wife*.

I don't think that really sank in until now. For better or for worse, we're tied together.

Everything has changed. I have his name. We had a wedding attended by every mafia boss in London. I won't be anonymous anywhere, ever again. My whole life I've been stuck in a tower, and today was jumping out, no idea if I have a parachute on.

The wet warmth of his seed is almost comforting in a way I can't explain. If coming beneath his tongue was the final out-of-body experience of a surreal day, then his come is a blanket keeping me safe.

Something soft and warm touches my chest, and I struggle to open my eyes. Orgasms always make me sleepy, but this is another level. Nikolai has a washcloth in his hand, and is leaning over me, carefully rubbing the dirty mess he made away. Over my breasts, my stomach, and down to between my legs, I'm wiped clean.

I accept it.

There's no way I could stop him. All my limbs are heavy and tingly. He doesn't demand anything of me. When he moves me up the bed, sweeps covers over me, and scoops me into his arms, I don't question that either.

I'm totally naked, and still a virgin. But I'm in his bed, and he holds me to him, one hand in my hair, the other around my waist, and brushing soft kisses over my face. My cheeks, my lips, my closed eyes. It's so sweet and lovely, his bare chest is rough hair and heated skin pressed to my breasts. Absolutely wrung out, I can't think why I shouldn't be enjoying this…

As I slip into unconsciousness, I remember.

For as long as we both shall live.

I was supposed to kill him…

Maybe tomorrow?

5

NIKOLAI

I knew she'd like the beach house in Cornwall. She was unsure on the journey here, just a quick trip in the jet and then the convertible I keep at the airfield. When we arrive at the old stone cottage with a big light-filled extension at the south side, like a butterfly she gravitates to the French doors and throws them open, walking out onto the decking.

Her sea-green dress is as insubstantial as everything I've seen her wear. Silk and skin. She's a creature made for comfort.

It's a bright but cool late summer day, and a breeze tugs at Lotte's hair as she stares out. The sky is blue, with knots of cloud chasing their leader to the east.

A seagull wheels and cries and the scent of salt is heavy in the air.

"Oh my god... I haven't..."

She hasn't been outside the tower in a long time, or London for even longer. She doesn't need to finish that sentence for me to understand. I don't tell her that I bought this house after seeing her use a background for her videos of a craggy clifftop with golden sand below.

She takes a deep, heaving breath, and darts around the deck and then down onto the lawn that slopes away to a low bank that hides a stone wall and an enticing gap.

"Does that lead to a beach?"

A glance behind is all the permission she asks for, and whatever she sees on my face—I can't be sure what it is because there's a tumult of emotions in my chest—reassures her, yes.

She hitches up her skirt and is gone, skipping down the steps. I bite my tongue.

I won't order her to be careful on the sandy stone. She's a grown woman. Wanting to be free comes with the risk of getting hurt, that's part of the appeal. So I follow right on her heels, ready to snatch her up if she stumbles, sharing her joy in this place I bought for her.

There are dozens of steps, descending to a small private beach hemmed in by cliffs that have tough plants clinging to them, defiantly putting out ragged little pink flowers and waving in the breeze.

We reach the bottom, and the sound of happiness she makes as she toes off her shoes and her feet touch the sand has me rearranging my cock in my trousers. Again.

She greedily takes in the view—the white foam, the grey-blue waves, the line of shells and seaweed and flotsam where the high tide dragged in its treasure.

And me? I observe my girl. Just as parched for her company as she has been for the outside world. Something in my soul relaxes seeing her excited and happy in the sunshine in a way not even her singing does.

I stuff my hands in my pockets as—skirt clinging to her legs in the breeze—she runs into the sea. The shriek at the cold and her giggle at the waves soaking the hem of her dress make me smile. But not as much as when she casts a glance over her shoulder at me and jerks her head.

"You can't go to the beach and not get in the water, Mr fancy Bratva boss Edmonton," she calls.

"Ah, I knew she was trouble," I say under my breath as I strip off my shoes and socks, then my suit jacket and tie, leaving them in a neat pile next to where she has haphazardly discarded hers.

I nominally roll up my trousers and I admit, the feel of sand beneath my feet is good. It's been too long of working too hard, and I'm going to make changes. If I can't take a day off to come to the beach, what exactly is the point of the blood I shed to be Edmonton's kingpin and protect Lotte? How will she know she's mine if I don't spend time with her in the fresh air, where she needs to be?

"A bit deeper, you've barely got wet," she teases when I stand, arms crossed, with the foamy water lapping at my toes.

"I'm not the one who gets wet, that's you."

She blushes, but she's still smiling as she dances over, hands outstretched towards me, beckoning. My cock responds with a throb of need.

Normally sex doesn't bother me either way. Desire is usually an itch I scratch with the nearest willing female. Before Rapunzel, I didn't care. I certainly never wanted to pursue a woman. But there's something about watching Lotte that sends blood surging to my cock. There's almost none of her body on show. No cleavage or upper thigh. But her way of looking at me...

She has no idea how close she is to being thrown over my shoulder, dumped onto the warm sand, and ravaged out here in the sunshine. She's at my mercy.

But I let her take my hands and draw me further into the sea.

"Lotte," I warn her as a little wave floods dangerously near to a suit my tailor will probably cry over if I ruin it with salty seawater.

"What?" She opens her eyes wide, the sun making glints of gold in the brown. "Big powerful mafia boss scared of a bit of sea?"

I roll my eyes. "No, but I—"

She takes her opportunity, flicking one dainty foot and splashing my trousers.

"Oops!" Her eyes sparkle with mischief.

I pretend to see something, turning away.

"What's this?" I point into the water, peering over it.

Curious creature that she is, she's straight to my side, leaning over where my hand hovers above the water's surface.

"Where? I can't—"

I slice my hand, propelling water right up into her face and she splutters, laughing even as she complains and futilely attempts to wipe herself dry. "No fair!"

"I don't play fair." I snatch up her hand and she tries to wheel away, pulling her to stand before me. "Don't move."

Releasing her, I ping out one cufflink and tug the shirt sleeve over my hand. Her gaze dips uncertainly as I cup the back of her head, my fingers sinking into her hair, and raise the fabric to her face.

"I'm going to dry your face," I tell her softly.

She doesn't reply, but surprise and perhaps disbelief creases her brow as I wipe all the droplets carefully away. Then we're standing in the sea, her warm hair impossibly silky over my hand, my shirt ruined with salt, my trousers soaked, and tension crackling between us.

It's irresistible.

"I'm going to kiss you."

She stares up at me, eyes big, still no words. I take that as a yes. I draw her closer with smooth movements she can see. No surprises. I'm learning about how flighty my ptichka is.

My phone trills.

She startles.

Fuck.

I try to ignore it, but the damage is done. She's withdrawn.

"You should get that. Might be important."

This time, when she steps away, I let her, yanking my phone out and answering Mikhail's call with a snapped, "What?"

Barefoot, Lotte clambers over rocks as I answer Mikhail's panicky questions. She's so damn cute as she kneels and peers into a rockpool.

A fight has broken out between some low-level Tottenham and Edmonton goons. Something lewd that my men were taunting the Tottenhams about, in a pub of all places. Idiots. I grind my teeth, since I can ill afford more losses in my ranks after my recent bloodbath. But as Mikhail tells me how Edmonton men mocked the Tottenham bastards about their kingpin shafting the Tottenham Princess, I see red.

"Bring them in, and shoot them."

Mikhail is silent, then, "Yes boss."

He thinks I'm overreacting. I am, and I don't care. "I thought I made myself clear: no disrespect to *my wife*."

"Yes, boss." He audibly swallows.

"We're allied with Tottenham now," I say mildly as I

watch Lotte. She bounces off the rocks onto the sand, strolling towards me. "Ensure no one forgets again."

"Yes—"

I hang up.

"Having a nice beach day?" Rapunzel has told me that she hasn't been to the seaside for years. That she misses it.

She nods, but there's a reservation. "My mum used to take me to the beach, and we'd hang out. Just the two of us. And Antonio, too. Our bodyguard."

Bodyguard? Does she not know that he was her mother's lover?

I can't share this with her. Obviously. Lotte smiles a little wistfully. "But I wish I could do a video. You know. For my silly little social media channel."

6

LOTTE

I'm having the best day with my enemy. The perfect day, and I know it's pathetic, but I want to share it with the people who have lifted me up through the loneliest times. Especially because I usually speak with ListeningToHer every day, I feel bad that they might be worried when I'm enjoying myself.

I try to act careless as I scuff my feet in the sand.

"It's not silly." He takes out a phone from his pocket.

"Sure you don't think it's silly," I scoff. "That's why you taunted me with it at the restaurant."

I left my phone and a bag of possessions in the car that brought me to the church—it's not like my wedding dress had pockets—and that was the last time I saw it. I doubt I ever will again, given my husband's security obsession.

"I've been meaning to give this to you." He holds out the phone.

What? That's not his phone, or mine. I notice he doesn't answer my barb about the restaurant. But even so, my eyes go wide. A new phone for me? "Is it tracked?"

He shrugs. "You know I've been listening—keeping an

eye on," he corrects himself, "everything that happens online at Tottenham Tower."

Listening?

But he's giving me a phone. It's not like he wasn't aware of my secret account. He neither confirms nor denies whether the phone is bugged, I notice. I'm not certain what that means, but I take the device from his proffered hand.

"What else did you hear?" I mutter, opening the phone. It has my favourite apps, all logged in already.

"Enough that I think you're better off out of there," he replies. "But I didn't know you were a prisoner."

"I wasn't a prisoner," I protest half-heartedly, trying to be a good, loyal daughter. Family is all, I remind myself. But it's a lie.

I called myself Rapunzel. When I tried to leave, my father locked me in my bedroom for a week, and he's cuffed me around the back of the head enough times when it looked like I was trying to speak privately with someone in a Tottenham Tower bar or shop that I know to duck out of the way.

"My father was protecting me from Edmonton. From *you*." See? I am loyal.

"Worked out well," Nik replies dryly.

I glare at him. Yeah. He just has to rub it in that we lost. I focus on the phone. He's given it to me; I'm going to speak to my friends. Online friends, but eh, I take companionship and praise where I can.

Opening the camera, I point it towards myself at the full stretch of my arm, trying to find the right angle. Normally I use a phone mount on a table, and film myself in my bedroom against a plain cold blue wall. I'm struggling a bit without my setup. Virtual backgrounds are convenient, if not as good as reality.

"You want me to film you?" he offers casually.

"I can do it." I don't need his help. I don't.

I fumble with the phone for a few minutes as he waits patiently, one eyebrow quirked up cynically.

Stopping, I sigh. "Why would you do that for me? What would you want in return?"

For a second, I imagine affection flares in his expression, but it's brief. Shuttered again before I can understand. He holds out his hand. "Not everything has a price."

I scoff. In the mafia world of secrets and lies, that's just not true. If it were, I would have companionship and love that I've never had... Except I do. From one place and person in particular. ListeningToHer doesn't put a price on their friendship with me. Even when occasionally my other fans are demanding, they're always patient.

"It's weird." This whole talking about my videos out loud rather than tapping on my phone. "No one else knows about Rapunzel." I'm used to keeping my recordings deniable, furtive. The idea of having someone else watching is disconcerting.

"It's our secret."

Nik can keep his word. Somehow, I know that, deep in my gut. I cross the gap towards him. My thumb brushes over his wrist as I pass him the phone and I think he doesn't notice, or that he isn't affected by the sparks that the touch causes because he's observing me fixedly, no response.

"I like for the sea's horizon—" I begin to explain how I frame my shots.

"I know."

He says it so confidently, I can't help but obey. The sunlight gleams off his black hair, highlighting it gold. He shakes his head, and a lock of hair falls almost over his eye, and I have the shocking urge to sweep it aside.

"You watched my videos?" I guess I thought he wouldn't have bothered. He's gorgeous and way older than me. Why would my little warbling attempts interest him?

One nod, then he gives a silent countdown with his fingers.

I panic, not ready as the red light indicates he's started the video.

But the words come stronger than I expect, clearer. I look right at my new husband and sing about being free. Instead of looking into the camera as I usually do, I hold his gaze as I belt out the words. I thought it was a pointed remark to sing about freedom when it came into my head. But it doesn't feel like that now. It's almost like a thank-you.

Which is ridiculous.

He doesn't watch the screen. The phone is forgotten and I'm singing for him, good chills going down by my back as we look at each other. He's as compelled by me as I am by him.

I draw out the last note and desperately try to come up with something to say to my followers. I can't. My whole mind is full of my husband.

"Hope you like the background for this one," I say after a beat, my brain stuttering into life. ListeningToHer, my most loyal and kind fan, will like this one, I think. The thought makes me smile.

"I like this real beach more." Nikolai passes me the phone and this time I'm careful to not allow our fingers to touch.

He's the enemy and he killed my mother. I have to remember her words—that family is everything. Blood ties.

I turn away and collapse onto the warm sand, the sun on my back as I edit the video so I'm anonymous but cute.

Out of the corner of my eye I watch my husband, calmly reclining nearby.

Then all of a sudden, like a fire is lit under him, he yanks his phone from his pocket, just as I begin to upload my video.

Weird.

It goes live and I sit with the phone in my lap, sharing my attention between the screen and the waves crashing and skidding over the rocks at the side of the beach, waiting for ListeningToHer. They always post a comment immediately, like they have an alert set up.

I wait. And wait.

My heart sinks as the minutes tick by.

"Huh." They're not listening, I guess. Maybe they've lost interest. My throat goes tight. Alone again. That little social media account has been my lifeline. That one relationship.

"What is it?" Nik asks.

"Oh nothing." It has to be nothing. Gah. I'm so stupid.

I hand the phone to him, and he pockets it.

"I just thought someone would comment on my video, and they didn't. I guess they're busy, and it's only a song." I'm proud of how stable my voice is.

"I'm sure he doesn't feel that way." My husband looks out at the horizon.

I raise my eyebrows. "How do you know they're a man?"

He's silent. Huh. Typical. He just assumed. Default male.

"You don't," I finish.

"Come on." He stands and offers his hands to help me up. "Time for lunch."

"We have to climb all those steps?" I didn't really consider that when I skipped down to the beach.

"Yep."

"Ugh. Well, I'll need all the boost I can get." I accept his hand, and he pulls me to my feet, but not into his arms, just holding my fingertips. I don't know how I feel about that.

"An escalator would spoil the ambience, don't you think?"

My lips twitch. He's kind of funny.

"Turn."

He releases me and I obey, trying not to notice how easy that is. To do what he says. To be his obedient wife. He gently brushes the sand off the back of my dress, and I refuse to notice how my bottom feels beneath his palm.

This is an impersonal brush.

What if he spanked me? I don't want to like that idea, but my body doesn't care. It responds to him, lighting up.

The effort taken to thank him and walk away rather than grabbing him and pulling him down on top of me is painful.

But not as painful as the steps. Man.

Behind me, Nik is barely breathing heavily, and halfway up the cliff I'm a red sweaty mess.

My throat is dying. On fire. Despite the humiliation, I have to stop.

"Want a push or shall I carry you?" he asks.

I snort. "Carry. You can't carry me up there."

In answer, he tips me into my arms. I catch sight of his smug grin as I yelp and cling to his neck.

"Are you nuts? Put me down before we both fall off the cliff!" My heart is hammering even harder now, blood racing through my veins. He's close. And holding me so easily.

"What? Because you're so heavy, ptichka?" He resumes climbing the steps.

That name. If Russian weren't an impossible language and a baffling alphabet, I'd have looked it up already. What does it mean?

It doesn't matter. It can't.

"Yes."

Oh god. His hands on my body are making me heat anew. This time with desire that bounces low in my belly. I hide my face in his neck. "And you'll see that I'm red in the face and sweaty."

"Just the way I like you." Nik grips me more tightly and I melt.

My dress has rucked up and his forearm presses to the backs of my knees. Every place where we touch is a relief, as if my whole body has been waiting to be in contact with him again. So when we reach the top and I wriggle and protest, I'm reluctant to be put down. And he hesitates as though he enjoys holding me too. He slides me down his body, and my hip rubs over an unmistakable hard bulge.

He has an erection. My mind can't take it in.

"Thanks." I smooth my dress self-consciously as I attempt to find my balance on the dense sandy lawn.

"Anytime."

He motions for us to go into the house with a tilt of his head, catching my fingers as we walk, making my heart pound, despite him being the one who carried me up all those steps. He's hardly out of breath.

Is it weird I find that really hot?

In the light kitchen he slides the glass doors so it's open to the outside, and maybe he always does that, but it helps. That and the grass just there, the steps and the beach, the horizon unimpeded by skyscrapers or smog.

He pulls tapas from the fridge and makes a joke that the housekeeper is a gem. I'm not super familiar with this sort of thing—my father is very formal—but I help get plates and bowls from the cupboard. A pair of each. One for him and one for me. We work around each other instinctively. It's sweetly domestic, playing house. The beach cottage is small, and if I ignore my conscience—I'm going to kill him, right?—I can imagine this is normal for us.

He suggests eating on the terrace, and while the wind tugs at my hair like a playful puppy, I ask him about himself. We miss out on all the mafia stuff. No word of family. No questions about who lived and died on the paths that brought us here.

When we've eaten our fill, he brings out ice cream and we lounge all afternoon, looking out at the sea. Just food and music. The conversation meanders comfortably to our favourite books and movies. A few in common, many not, and I'm exclaiming that he must read this, or I'm going to make him watch that.

I'm not going to. The fact he will never read anything I've recommended to him is a weight in my stomach.

There's a thread of awareness that shimmers between us and as the sun dips, I can't help myself. I find excuses to touch him. A speck of dust on his shirt. Fingertips to his knee when he makes a joke. So when he casually offers his hand, palm up, between us, I first brush my fingers against his in a deniable, movement. Then when he loosely clasps his big hand around mine, I don't draw away. I lace our hands together and take in the warmth.

And the thought drifts across my mind like a fluffy cloud: much more of this fresh air, infinite sky, and the reassurance of Nik's bulky presence and I'll fall for him.

It's an act. I know that, and I'm acting myself, right?

Right?

I wish my heart knew that, because it's insisting today has been magic. The best day of my life.

It's only when I go into the beach house to nip to the loo, the door closing behind me with a click, that my chest tightens. The air inside is still, and it's like the wind-blown salt and sand that carried me back here drops into my stomach.

I'm going to end up trapped. Again.

After being locked up for years, I confess, today has been... amazing. Yes because of the beach and feeling free. The air that isn't recycled a million times, the breeze on my face and tangling my hair. I knew being away from Tottenham Tower and London would be wonderful.

I didn't have *liking my husband* on my bingo card, but here we are.

My husband.

My enemy. The man who gave me an orgasm so intense I basically had an out-of-body experience, then kissed me and held me all night.

My videographer.

My personal chef. Sort of.

My mother's *murderer*.

And while I can forgive his smug gorgeousness on the beach thing, am I really ready to give up revenge?

Being with Nikolai is like hearing a half remembered favourite song. Every part of me wants to lean into him and sing at the top of my voice.

I could easily fall in love with him. I'm not sure I haven't already begun to tumble because being with him is too easy, but that doesn't change the facts. It's Edmonton who killed my mother and the mafia war that gave my father the excuse to keep me locked up. He always said Tottenham Tower had everything I needed. A cinema, two pools, a gym, cafés and restaurants, and a nightclub.

I guess it makes me greedy, but I need trees and salt air, sand between my toes and to go wherever I want to go at a whim.

There's a sly voice in my brain that says Nik—my husband—will provide *all* of that, plus orgasms that send my heart pattering and make me weak.

And that's the problem, isn't it? What kind of daughter am I if I fall for my mother's killer? The only person who cared about me, and he all but confessed to her murder.

This cage of Nikolai's is better, prettier, bigger. But I'm returning to being trapped. There's only one thing to do.

I have to kill him before I lose my nerve.

7

NIKOLAI

"Come out to the terrace," I invite as she emerges from the house, pale. It's being inside. She doesn't like being trapped. She needs light and space and air, same as the little caged bird I called her.

"But..."

Drinks and laughter and watching the sunset over the calm blue ocean with her in my arms. I can't stop touching her since I carried her up the stairs, and she is finding ways to draw closer too. Like she broke open a dam by taking my hand.

"Why don't you show me the bedroom?" she blurts out.

I look at her speculatively. It's odd. This is the third time she's been over-eager about getting me into bed.

She presses her lips together and regards me from beneath her eyelashes, looking shy and impatient and a bit nervous. That agitation seems genuine enough. Perhaps I'm seeing problems where there are none.

But even so, there's no need for any hurry. We're going to do this on my schedule, and she's my wife, so I can play a slow game of seduction.

I want her. Of course I can't wait to have her come again. I'm longing for the feel of virgin pussy on my cock.

But I have the experience to know that a pleasure anticipated and savoured is all the sweeter.

"There's time. But unlike the London mafia bosses, the police, banks, politicians, every man who works for me, and half of London, I can't make the sun wait for you," I tease.

She pauses for just long enough to make me suspicious, but then the relief that is undisguised on her face removes my doubts. Whatever she's worried about—maybe that she thinks I'm going to jump on her and paw her like an animal before she's wet and desperate for me—it's not happening.

I tuck her into my side when she comes to stand close enough we're touching, and she fits as though she was designed to be sheltered by me. Or I was designed to be nestled into by her.

My arm rests lightly on her shoulders and I indulge in threading my fingers into her hair as the colours get more and more intense. We watch silently, my skin tingling with awareness of her, her eyes trained on the sky as the sun dips below the horizon and the darkness fades to grey-blue.

It's a small step, but she has come close voluntarily.

There's still a question in my mind about her earlier behaviour though, and I have a way of discovering more.

"You can stay outside. Make a video." I indulge in dropping a kiss on the top of her head and slip her new phone into her hands before disappearing into the house.

Inside, I switch on the string lights, and she looks up at them, delight brightening her face. They cast a golden glow over the decking, and above the night sky is just beginning its display. After nipping upstairs to open all the windows— I've noticed how that helps her—in the kitchen I turn my back and switch on my phone. My smile can't be suppressed when I see that video she posted. The one we created together.

> ListeningToHer: Love the backdrop and your singing is gorgeous, as ever. But more than that, it's nice to see you looking happy. Were you?

I watch her in the fading light as the stars shimmer into existence. She tilts her head right up, staring at the sky as though she's never seen them before. Those stars were always there, of course. Just maybe she couldn't see them from Tottenham Tower, with all the surrounding glow from the city. The darkness reveals the light.

I indulge in watching her for a few minutes, until it occurs to me that perhaps she needs to think I'm distracted and not paying her attention in order to talk with her friend. I busy myself in the kitchen, figuring out what to make her to eat. I hadn't planned on staying the night here, but it's so obvious she's happier outside of London, there's no question about returning.

It takes only a few minutes and then when I check again —thank god I managed to turn off the alert on the beach in time, I was sure I was about to give myself away totally— there's a message from her.

> Rapunzel: I'm so glad you liked the video! And yeah, I was happy.

> ListeningToHer: Good. You deserve it, little songbird.

> Rapunzel: You're too kind to me.

> ListeningToHer: Never. You make it easy. I hope you have many more happy days.

> Rapunzel: Me too. There was something
> about today, though. A magic.

Yeah. She's right.

I can't even remember the last time I was so relaxed. I wonder if she's thinking this day is special because she's escaped Tottenham Tower, is outside of London, or at the beach. Or whether she has realised that this is *us*.

Surely she can see the difference? She had weeks of wedding planning when she was free to come and go and buy herself anything she wanted.

She doesn't make a new video, but I hear the faint melody as she listens to the one we took today. When I glance out at her, she's looking away. Putting aside her phone, she shivers.

A thread of discomfort rubs at me. Is it a betrayal to pretend to be someone else? Just her friend when I want so much more.

Her shiver doesn't last long. Along with toasted cheese sandwiches, a bowl of brightly coloured salad with plenty of the good stuff, and a plate of chocolate truffles, I bring out a furry cream blanket slung over my arm.

I wrap it over her shoulders before flicking her nose, softening the affection with playfulness. "Can't let you get cold, can we."

She leans into me, so I pull her onto the wooden bench to sit beside me at the table, just touching. It's so casual. Natural. I can't tell if she feels the warmth emanating between us.

I make no apology for the simple food, and I don't suggest we go inside. Lotte eats the greasy food ravenously.

As we eat, I tell her about beaches I've been to that I think she'll like when I take her—Thailand, Croatia, Chile, and South Africa—and her eyes go dreamy as she listens. I try to describe what I imagine: the long sand stretching away, the sun, the waves. The two of us, together. That I'll take her to these places, and she'll stare at the distant horizon, stained with a pink and blue sunset, and we'll be a couple.

And that's when I see a flicker of something dark in her eyes. I'm reminded that to her, this is an arranged mafia marriage, and she is a prize of war.

When the food is nothing but buttery streaks and coco powder on the plates, and the limp bits of lettuce left in the bowl, I bring out hot mugs of tea and the conversation lapses into relaxed pauses.

She holds out, but eventually rests her head on my shoulder. And I enjoy her trust far too much, stroking her hair.

"Come on. Sleep time," I say into her ear.

"Yes. Yes, right." She stumbles and shakes a bit. "Let's go in."

Inside the house she seems okay, but when I approach her after closing the massive glass sliding doors, she's frozen.

Like she can't move for fear of what I might do. Or not do.

Oh shit.

I restrain a sigh of frustration. We're back to square one.

"I'll sleep on the sofa if you'd be more comfortable," I say, coming to a stop before her where she stands in the middle of the lounge. "There's no hurry."

"Nik, you said if I begged..."

My eyebrows raise. This is a sudden turn around.

"I want you. Please." She reaches out and grabs my

shirt, pulling herself in. For a second, I don't move. This is so nearly right, so almost what I crave.

Every atom in my body is demanding that I just take this at face value. Even as I can't resist, as my arms come up to encompass her, kiss her, holding the nape of her neck and stroking my tongue hungrily on hers. She tastes sweet and heady. I'm high on this kiss and the heat that has shimmered between us all day flares arousal right into my cock.

I retain just enough sanity to draw back and look into her eyes. There's doubt there, but desire too, and she nods. Touching our foreheads together, I breathe in her strawberries and vanilla scent. I'm helpless to resist her.

"I promised if you begged, and I'm a man of my word. Come."

On the stairs, the air is a little stale, and she tenses. Probably just because this house isn't lived in all the time. Her breathing goes erratic, but as we step into the bedroom, and she sees the open full-length windows leading to a balcony, it evens out again.

The room is shrouded in shadows and lit by moonlight, and I release her to let her explore. The massive bed to one side, an expanse of shimmering carpet, and beside a discreet wall that presumably leads to an en suite, there's a freestanding bath, roll-topped, pointing to view the ocean.

I flick on a light and settle on the edge of the bed, watching.

There's lust here, yes. She can't fake that. But something else too. Because she's trying to distract and seduce me. It's working. My cock is an iron bar as she pulls her dress over her head in one swift movement, leaving her white lace knickers and matching bra.

"So beautiful." I beckon her to me. I don't know what

she's planning, but I don't think it has to do with Tottenham. Not after the way her father treated her.

She slips her fingers into the hem of her knickers, still too far away to touch, and a bit shy. Her movements are slow when I'm growing more impatient by the second.

"Now, ptichka."

8

LOTTE

Sexy. Alive. Strong. The best version of myself. That's me, as I shimmy to him. I'm a cocktail of poison, happiness, mania, sexual high, and thrumming fear. Just before I'm within his reach, I unclip my bra and pull it off. It's not elegant, because I'm nervous and I have to run my hand over where the blade is hidden.

I discard the bra in as casual a way as possible, on the bed. Then I'm in his arms, pulled onto his lap, and his mouth is on mine. I melt, physically. I dissolve. It takes all my effort to retain the tiniest bit of mental clarity as I remove his clothes.

It's a tussle, as Nik only wants to pleasure me. He has his hands making the sweetest mischief all over my body.

He chuckles as I struggle with his cufflinks, snapping them off for me when I make an incoherent sound of frustration. For some reason he has to be naked for this. Why, I can't remember, but it's critical.

There's no time to pause and admire his chest as I manage to get his shirt off. It's all a blur of his musky scent, his hands, the desperation, and conflict to not be drugged by his kisses.

I fumble with his belt and my vision blurs. Shit, am I going to cry? I'm not. No way.

Nik covers my hands with his and the stillness means I realise I'm shaking.

"Are you sure?" he asks, low and intense. I don't meet his eyes, but I can feel his gaze on me.

"Yes. I'm certain." I am. I have to be.

Every part of me sings that this is right.

This act is easy.

That's because it's not fake, a little voice whispers. I shove the voice back into its box. It isn't real. I can't be in love with Nik. Wait, when did he become Nik and not the enemy or Nikolai?

I mean I want him. Not love, that's—no. This helium balloon in my chest isn't love.

He lets me pull his trousers and boxers off in one, and I'm unhinged, pushing him down on the bed. On his back, looking up at me, he ought to seem vulnerable. But he's running his hands over me as I crawl over him and I'm desperately aware that I'm slight compared to his muscled body. He's hard everywhere.

"My perfect wife," he murmurs, reaching up and smoothing my hair away from my face. He smiles as it falls straight back, a wall of tendrils that mean I don't have to look him in the eyes. I just give in to the urges of my body, and settle myself over him. My wet slit on the solid length of his cock.

He groans, and although a whimper escapes me simultaneously, I'm holding on. I shift my hand until I find my bra, even as I lean down and kiss him.

Tears prickle behind my eyelids. I screw them shut as I

release the blade from its hiding place and before I can change my mind, I bring it to his throat.

As the cold metal touches his skin, everything stops.

Silence.

I open my eyes and draw my head back to find him watching me.

One breath.

Two.

I will myself to do it. My hand doesn't move.

For my mother. For freedom.

But I'm held by those silver eyes. Neither of us moves.

"Don't do this, ptichka," he murmurs, careful and quiet as if I were a wild animal he's taming. "Give yourself to me instead."

For a second, I let myself imagine it. Dropping the knife and all my principles.

"I can't." I'm naked on top of this amazing, terrifying, deadly man, and I've hesitated in my one goal. By all measures he should already be dead. The metal is right by the artery in his neck, pulsing just under the skin.

One press.

I have to.

But the press I make isn't with my hand. It's my hips, down onto the flat of his cock.

"I'll give you everything," he continues in a rough whisper. "All the freedom you want and all the love you can take. You're brave and resilient, and I respect that. I'm on your side."

"You killed my mother." Firmer ground here. My hand isn't steady, but I can do this, even caught as I am in his eyes.

"My hands are soaked in blood, yes," he says, low and easy. "But not hers, ptichka."

I don't believe him. I can't.

"What the hell does that mean? Ptichka." My hand is shaking now, and the knife slices into the skin of his neck. A trail of red slides down to the pillow.

Well. I said it wouldn't be my virgin blood on the sheets. I was right.

He chuckles. "You want to know, do you?"

"Whatever," I mutter petulantly. "I'll google it once you're dead."

But I don't kill him. I look into his eyes and wish things were different.

"It means little bird. It's a Russian endearment."

Right. Well, that was an anti-climax. He was using a generic term of affection. Nothing special.

I am going to kill him. I am. As soon as I remember the last time anyone called me anything but Charlotte or Rapunzel or...

"But you could also translate it as little songbird."

Oh my god.

There's only one person who calls me *their little songbird*.

"You're..."

"Yes." He reaches up, oh so slowly, clasps my hand and brushes his thumb over my knuckles, then moves the knife from his throat as I'm in shock. My husband is the one person who I've relied on and has believed in me. He's the first to compliment me on my latest songs, or commiserate when I've let my mask slip and revealed my loneliness.

"I've been listening to you all along."

I'm so entranced by the idea of him caring for me, I've forgotten his other sins. I tighten my grip on the knife.

Revenge. There's still revenge for my mother. However sweet he was to me, that doesn't mitigate against murder. I take a breath, strengthening my resolve, and go to stab him in the gut.

But as I move, he does too, snatching my hand and pinning it above my head. I reach for his eyes, to scratch and claw, and my knees come up, hard and fast.

He's too quick. My other arm is wrenched up, and his thighs cover mine, pressing me into the bed.

I'm trapped. Both of my wrists are in one of his hands, and he's heavy on top of me, my core exposed, my breasts naked and his rough chest hair rubbing on my nipples. His hard length is bearing down onto my stomach and my legs are spread by his.

With his free hand, he brushes his knuckles over my cheek.

"Now, little songbird. Listen to me."

9

NIKOLAI

It takes her a second, but she realises she's caught.

"You arsehole," she spits.

Despite her struggling, she can't get away and she doesn't use the knife still clutched in her fingers. She could cut my hands, but is deciding not to. My cock is pressed right onto her most sensitive flesh. And she's so wet. Deliciously turned on.

"Are you going to rape me?" The words and her eyes are defiant, but there's a thread of fear in her voice. A tremor.

"My beautiful girl. As though I'd let you off so easily. I've told you before, if you want my cock, you'll have to beg. All this cream is a good start." I flex my hips, shifting against her to emphasise how slippery it is between us, then reach up to her forehead and stroke my thumb over her downy hairline. "But I need your mind too. Your pretty words. You have to tell me you can't live another minute without me inside you."

"I won't break."

Not the way I'd put it, but there you go. "You will."

I pray I'm right. I love her far too much to release her.

"I hate you." But she can't even find the anger to say it with conviction. It's more wistful, and as she writhes beneath me, her eyes shut momentarily, and I realise it's from her beaded nipples rubbing on the rough hair of my chest.

Lowering my head, I swipe my lips over hers. She yields for a fraction of a second before clamping her lips together.

"I didn't kill your mother." I draw back so she can see the truth in my expression.

She snorts. "You spied on me. You played me. I don't know what your game is, Edmonton, but I don't believe you."

My game? It's so simple. The game of love. I want to win her heart.

"What makes you so certain?" My body is still responsive to her, even as we talk. My cock clamours to slip inside her. But I hold back. Her trust has to come first.

"You told me. You said your brother went the same way as my mother. Killed because of the mafia feud."

I shake my head. "Killed by someone they should have been able to depend on. That was the similarity. I was telling your father I knew."

She blinks and scowls. "Tottenham killed your brother."

And I notice that she doesn't say "we" anymore. She's disassociated herself from her family's mafia already. I wonder if her loyalty has shifted, without her even recognising it.

I pause. Will she be disgusted by what I've done to protect her? How far my obsession goes?

Ignoring the implied question about my brother, I say mildly, "Tottenham hasn't been capable of that for a while."

"Gloating now, are you? You killed my mother, maybe you shouldn't be so proud of yourself."

"No, I didn't."

She scoffs. "Sure. Or one of you Edmonton bastards did, anyway."

"Not me, nor any of Edmonton," I reply patiently. Fuck but she's a temptation beneath me. My body is held by my self-control on the edge of arousal. "I don't do that, Lotte. Removal of evidence isn't my style. Accidents, or outright shootings, but I didn't have any way to mourn my parents properly. I wouldn't deny that to anyone else."

"Oh." She chews her lip. "You want me to think someone in Tottenham murdered her?"

"Not *someone*. Your father."

"That's ridiculous." But there's no conviction at all in it. "How would you know something like that even if it were true?"

"I was the digital spy for Edmonton for two decades." Nothing went on I didn't know about, except that she was imprisoned. I didn't know that, and I wish I had. "He killed her because she was having an affair with her bodyguard."

It's that moment that I see the pieces come together in her mind, like syncing music and lyrics. "Oh my god. My mother tried to tell me. Repeatedly."

Her eyes are full of sadness and betrayal. Carefully, I grasp the little makeshift blade in her hand, and she releases it. I toss it away before rolling onto my back and bringing her with me. I bring her hands down to nestle between our chests. Then, fingers crossed for foolhardy, I release her.

She doesn't move. "Antonio was my father. That was what she meant when she said blood and family are the most important thing."

Kissing her cheek, I extract my hands to lightly run up and down her back as she rearranges reality in her mind.

"That's why I don't look…" She hesitates. "Like David Tottenham."

She doesn't call him her father, I note. It makes more sense this way, and she knows it.

"I'm sorry, ptichka."

"He imprisoned me. He controlled me all this time and he isn't even my father."

My heart squeezes. I should have acted sooner. The extent of her captivity was a Tottenham secret not even I knew.

"He told me it was for my own protection."

"He's a liar. Men who can truly protect and satisfy the women they love have no need to keep them locked up."

"Or held down," she snips back at me.

"If you really wanted to escape or kill me, you'd have done it by now."

She swallows and I can tell she's thinking of the moments today that she flinched away from killing me, or was having too much fun to consider how vulnerable I'd left myself.

"You didn't stop me. Is that what your parents' marriage was like?" she asks in a small voice.

"Yes." And it's the kind of relationship I'll have with Lotte. One based on absolute trust, with no need for locks or chains.

"So what is this? Revenge for Tottenham killing your parents?"

I shake my head. "I'm done with the feud. I've gone to some trouble to end it with a marriage, if you recall."

"Tottenham was on the brink of financial collapse, even

before you took over." She levers herself up on my chest so she can see my face more clearly, and her hair falls over her shoulders in a gleaming dark waterfall. I run my hand through the silk of it—everything about her is a contrast of smooth and fire.

"Yes. I decided after my parents disappeared that I prefer warfare without bloodshed to those not actively involved. But I don't shy away. What's necessary is necessary."

"Your brother and uncle both died just before you took control of the Edmonton Bratva."

I guess I always knew this conversation would occur eventually. Betrayal of your own mafia is unthinkable in our world. It's the ultimate taboo, a sign of corruption beyond anything the mafias might do to each other. I can only hope she understands.

"I killed them."

Confusion creases her brow. "Both?"

I shrug. They could have lived if they had listened to me.

She shakes her head, but it's not denial now. It's disbelief and a little bit of... is that admiration? "Why?"

"My uncle was done with the feud too. But he had a very different solution to the one we came up with. He was going to bomb the tower."

"Tottenham Tower?" she echoes faintly.

My chest tightens at the thought, an echo of the fear that gripped me then. "I couldn't let that happen."

"Why not?" Her baffled expression pinches at my heart. "It was just Tottenham."

"Because I would never allow you to be hurt." It feels good to admit this. "I would sooner burn the whole of

London down than have you upset. Anyone who hurts you dies."

Her mouth falls open. There's a long pause. Then brown eyes meet mine.

She places her hands on my chest, right over my thumping heart. Then her nails dig in slightly. Possessive. "I spared your life, husband, so you owe me. I'm not letting you go now."

"Savage little songbird, aren't you?" We're done with mourning and sadness tonight. If she's claiming me, she'll find I'm not so tame. I grab her around the waist and flip her back over. Her landing is hard onto the mattress, but as she moves to protest, I'm on her. Covering her with my body, shoving a knee between hers and looking down into her face. She's breathless and the desire I see there makes my cock throb. I settle myself right on her soft folds, holding myself on my forearms and leaning down to brush a light kiss over her lips. It's a deliberate contrast to the way I'm trapping her firmly everywhere else.

She pushes up her hips, despite being thoroughly caught, the movement causes the head of my cock to notch at her entrance. A groan rips from my throat.

She's soaked.

Neither of us speaks, like we're not admitting this is happening. I scan her face for any signs that she's scared or uncomfortable. There's none.

Her expression is open, and her trust in me squeezes my heart.

"Is there anything else you need to discuss?"

She smirks. "The weather?"

"Anything that's keeping us apart," I growl. "Because I have to tell you, I'm very close to slipping into you and fucking you until you can remember nothing but the feeling of being taken by me. And it will be too late for regrets then."

She lets out a whimper and trembles.

"You're the one who's got me pinned to the bed at your mercy. You put me here. Don't think I haven't realised how you encouraged me to suggest making peace when we were talking on the video app, *my dangerous mafia boss husband.*" Each word is heavy, weighted.

She's soaked, dripping over the tip of my cock, and I swear she gets wetter as she describes me. Which bit does she like, I wonder? Because the word that made blood surge into my dick was *husband*. And *my*.

That ownership has certain privileges I'd like to avail myself of. Immediately.

"No more misunderstandings. Do you want to get pregnant?"

She hides for a second, turning her head to the side, and I can see her mind looking for the correct answer, the good girl answer that won't cause trouble.

"Look at me."

Her eyes snap to mine.

"The truth," I demand.

"Maybe?" she whispers. "I do. At some point."

"How about today?" I say softly. "How about we forget that blade you were going to put in me, and I fill you with seed instead, and make you round with my child."

Shock registers on her face. Disbelief. Then dawning happiness. "You'd like us to have a baby? I thought men didn't want—"

"Forget everything else, and know this: I love you and I'm going to keep you, protect you, make you mine over and over again. And I'm going to love and protect and provide for all of the kids I hope we'll have. So knowing that, I'll ask you again: do you want to get pregnant?"

"Yes." She nods like I might take away what she most wants. "Yes, I do."

"Good. Because I want nothing more than to be bare inside you. To fill you up with my come and make you mine."

She whimpers, going soft beneath my hands like what I've said makes her needy and hot, just as it makes me focused and hard. I want to breed my beautiful wife.

"My husband." And there's something like awe in her voice. "Make me yours."

"I will. I promise. You belong to me, brave little songbird. You're a survivor, you've been through a lot and now I'm going to take care of you. You're my wife now. Say you're my wife and that's where your allegiance lies. With me."

"You were ListeningToHer, all along?" she double checks. "You tracked me down, you basically stalked me, you plotted to get me into your bed, and killed anyone who tried to hurt me."

"Yes. And I'm not going to apologise for it." If that's where she's going with this—

"Then how can I not be loyal to you?"

The tension in my chest eases.

"My allegiance has been with you every minute since yours has been with me, Nik. You kept me sane. You supported me when I thought I couldn't go on. I *love* you."

My heart stops.

"You love me?" I assumed I'd have to wait far longer for her to return my love. Definitely for her to tell me she loved me.

She gulps, and nods, uncertainty in her expression, like she's worried that she's taken a step too far.

Ha.

She has no idea how far my obsession and love for her goes. It's more infinite than the stars.

"And do you trust me?"

A slow smile catches her lips and spreads across her face. "I trust you, husband. Take me."

10

LOTTE

"Say it again."

I stretch my arms up over the pillows in a gesture of surrender. "Please."

A growling purr rumbles from his chest as he lowers his head to where my breasts are exposed, pulled up high. A kiss makes me gasp, then he's laving, torturing, sending sparks over my skin and right down to where I'm aching with need for him.

"That's very good, ptichka," he murmurs as he gathers up my offered hands. He settles his weight over me, both my hands pinned by one of his, his chest over my breasts and his hips on mine. I wriggle my legs outwards, and tilt my hips until the rounded head of his hard cock is at my entrance, and his knees are between my thighs.

I'm utterly caught and it's the best feeling in the world.

My folds part as I writhe beneath him more. I'm desperately seeking more of him. And friction to my aching clit.

Nikolai's eyes narrow. "My perfect little slut, you're enjoying being held down, aren't you?"

"Yes," I admit.

"I'm going to thrust my whole cock into your virgin pussy as punishment. I will make you scream."

Arousal spikes from my belly to my throat.

"I'm yours." I want him so much. I need him close. Closer. I can't bear all the distance between us. I'd cut open my chest to put my beating heart against his if I could. Or if that was sane in any way, shape, or form.

But he *loves* me. He's been the one encouraging me and caring, making me smile and comforting me all along. I've been his little songbird from the moment we first messaged each other, and it's impossible to express with words how much ListeningToHer has been a part of the confidence that eventually led to insisting my father took me to meet with the head of Edmonton. Sure, Nik planted that thought. But he also fed the belief that I could do it when I had no reason to believe in myself.

"Tell me if it hurts," he whispers against my lips, as though he's sharing a secret, just between the two of us, hidden from our more ruthless selves, before silencing me with a hard kiss.

It's a kiss that allows no room for questions, until he lifts his head to stare into my eyes as he presses onto my folds, saying more loudly, "Take my big cock like a good girl."

I nod. Slowly, so slowly, he pushes in. He's clearly too large, and splitting me open. There's a pinch and OMG he's *too much*. He's going to make a permanent hole in me.

"You're so fucking tight." His free hand comes up to my cup my jaw, stroking over my lips tenderly before pushing into my mouth with his thumb.

I moan around his thumb, unable to contain myself as desire flares. It's so intimate. He's in my mouth and right at my core, driving to be closer.

"Not so much my wife as my little hussy, aren't you?" he teases. "Needy for your husband's cock."

My pussy releases. The pain goes and Nikolai slides deeper. The pressure, the fullness. Everything is so good. His cock leaves no room for doubt. There's just me and him and a future full of babies and laughter and days on the beach.

"That's it," he groans as I whimper. "Take it. You want me to fill you up until you don't know where you end and I begin, don't you?"

"Yes." I flex my hands against his grip, and close my lips around his thumb and suck. It sounds insane but I love that he's got me totally held. I don't have to take any responsibility for what's happening. There's no question about whether I'm doing it right, because he is doing this to me.

With his ability to read my emotions after so much time of us talking and him watching me, he dips his head and whispers into my ear, slipping his hand from my mouth. "Doing okay, ptichka? Does it hurt?"

"It's amazing," I reply, equally low, before nipping his ear. He chuckles and punches his hips forward, hard. Pleasure and pain flares from my pussy outwards then smooths as he eases back and thrusts again. I relish both. The next thrust is just pleasure as he opens me up.

This game is making me even hotter, winding me with more and more need.

He's hiding his gentle questions and caring words, partitioning them off from the dominant lover. My husband is huge and solid and hot inside me and with every gliding roll of his hips over me, each time he pushes me mercilessly into the mattress I want him more.

"You're taking all of me like such a good girl." He

smiles, feral and dangerous. "So you can have a treat. I'm going to take more. Open up."

He shifts one of my knees up, and I mirror the movement on the other side. I spread my legs wider and accept more of him, opening myself up completely.

"That's it. You're my best girl, so tight and wet. Trust me to make it good for you."

Keeping my hands trapped, he changes the angle of his hips, so the head of his cock is rubbing right at my entrance, over and over, as his hand explores one side of what of my body is exposed. The pushed-out swell of my breast, my waist, my hip. But it's the shallow thrust of his cock that's driving me wild, stimulating parts of me which were dormant before he discovered them.

It's good, so good, winding me up and up, but not quite enough, and when he adjusts again, thrusting further in, I sob at the change. It's more satisfying, and I love it, but I need that spiralling pleasure.

"Who owns you?" he demands, releasing my hands to hold himself up on one forearm and reaching down with the other. His breath is hot on my lips, his body heavy, brutal almost with every thrust.

"You." I can feel him at my belly button. He's rearranging my insides and adding a physical joining to how our hearts are combined, and our lives now that he's my husband.

"I own you. You're mine to please." He crams his fingers between our bodies in the space between thrusts, further and further, patient, until the push becomes a slide from the moisture seeping out from me. Then he's stroking my clit in circles and watching my eyes, a greedy expression on his face. And I ignite. I don't know how he's doing it. Maybe the combination of me being insanely turned on, and him being thick and hard, rubbing just the right spot. I'm surrounded by him, his weight over me, his cock inside me, and his fingers pressing my clit in a way that has me on the edge of coming, the pleasure stacking up.

"Tell me. Scream it," he growls into my ear. "I want everyone to know I own you. Your beautiful body. Your heart. Your soul." He keeps up the rhythm of his body into mine, playing me.

"You do!" It's a sob. "You own me. Nikolai, oh!" And that is as much verbalisation as I can manage before I come. The release is a shuddering, rolling, white heat through my body, from my clit all the way to my toes.

He coaches me through the pleasure, whispering sweet words of love and affection that I barely hear through the rush of blood.

"Oh god," I breathe. "That was…"

"Nope," he says with smug amusement. "Your *husband*."

"Oh husband," Laughter erupts from my chest. "Oh. My. Husband."

"Ptichka." He grins and rolls us over, so I'm laid on him, boneless from the orgasm that is still singing in my blood. Because he's magic, his hard cock is wedged right where I need him. An anchor. "Hearing you laugh is almost as good as feeling you come on my cock."

"Really?" I rub my face on his chest, the soft skin a delicious contrast with his light scattering of black hair.

"Yep." It's only then I notice he's piling the pillows at his back, so he is moving us so I'm sitting on his lap.

"Now, wife." He gathers up my hair in his hands and tugs. I gasp as the slight pinpricks and the tightening on my scalp sends pleasurable shivers all down my spine. My head tilts back, even as I lean into him, chasing the sensation of my hair being pulled.

"Such a delightful slut," he says affectionately, forcing my gaze to his silver one. How did I ever think his eyes were stone? They're full of mirth and love, and I can see that it was determination, not hostility, that made his eyes grey rather than silver when we first met in person.

"I need to feel you come on my cock again. You can do one more for me before I fill you up. And this time, I want you to do it."

"What?" I'm barely conscious after he threw me off that cliff of pleasure. I'm pretty sure my role here is as a receptacle for his come, not to have more orgasms, and definitely not to have any active task.

His eyes have gone charcoal grey, serious and dark.

"Do you trust me?" He swallows even as he continues to stroke in and out slowly, tilting his chin as though he's confident in my answer, but there's still a shadow there.

Uncertainty about whether I've really understood that he's in this, and so am I.

It's a line I want to scrub out.

"I do." And this I do feels more significant than the one I said in the church. Because I mean it. I trust him absolutely.

"Then ride me."

11

NIKOLAI

In my filthiest dreams about Lotte—and there were many, and they were dirty as fuck—I never imagined anything half as good as this. I thought she would be restrained, nervous. I did not consider she'd be a tigress who tried to eat me whole.

Her brown eyes gleam gold in the soft light as she takes my challenge and interprets it in her own way. She places her hands on my shoulders and lifts herself up, bringing her sweet little tits right to my mouth. I'd take advantage of that if I weren't distracted by my cock slipping out with a wet pop, and her scowl.

Instantly I regret this. I want her back on me, tight and soaking.

"It's okay," I reassure her, even though it's not. It's torture. I need to feel her come again. Her pleasure is the most important thing to me, because when she's coming, a scream on her lips, and her body doing as I will it, she's *my* toy. I'm giving her that pleasure, no one else.

But to do that, I want full access to my girl. Her breasts, her clit, the whole damn lot. And I want her to know she's as in control of this as she needs to be. She did, after all, try to murder me to get freedom. Our marriage will always provide her with more than that option.

I take my cock in my hand and cup her bottom—hell is there anything sweeter than this woman's arse?—and line us up.

"Go on. Use me."

Her hair is mussed from me pounding her into the bed, falling over her shoulders and sticking out a bit at the side. She's never looked more beautiful. Nothing could compare to the flush over her neck and the glow in her cheeks, and the way she's biting her lip as she concentrates.

She grips my shoulders in her little hands and eases down. As her wet folds touch the helmet of my cock the pleasure spreads down.

"Your bare, swollen pussy is so perfect."

"You're so big," she sighs and yeah, I don't mind that.

An inch down and she feels amazing.

"You were made to take me. You can do it."

Her nails dig into my muscles as she slides the rest of the way down.

"Make yourself come." I need her to come so hard she's shaken to her core. I'm going to reduce her to a quivering wreck of a girl. The power and intimacy of her orgasming on my cock, from my touch, is exactly the sort I crave. "Make me come inside you and give you a baby."

A nod from her, and I cup her tit, pinching her nipple as she eases herself up and down, getting her bearings, gaining confidence.

"I'm going to do this to you every day for the rest of our lives," I promise her. "I'm going to make you cry with how good it is, until you beg me for mercy because you can't come yet again."

Smoothing my hand down her body, I luxuriate in her softness.

When I get to her mons, I slide lower, between her legs and she throws her head back and cries out. "Yes."

"Where are you going to come?"

"On your cock," she gasps out, then makes a keening noise as I rub over her clit, where she needs it.

"And where am I going to come?"

"Inside me." This time it's a squeak.

"Yes, right up against your womb. I'm going to breed you. I want a nest full to bursting." Her thighs slap against mine, and my balls tighten. I can't last much longer. She feels too damn good as I press my fingers into her soft flesh, holding her hard enough to leave bruises as I lift and pull her onto my cock repeatedly.

I almost hope it bruises, to join her ring as a sign of my ownership. My marks all over her body. I want everyone to know she belongs to me.

I give in and thrust upwards, deeper, and harder and she whimpers, thrashing.

"Give it to me." I circle her clit with my thumb. "Give me one more orgasm and I'll fill you up."

Her eyelids flutter. Fuck she's so beautiful as she's lost in pleasure.

I look at where my cock rams into her, where she's taking it all, and arousal spikes through me, a sweet, heady drug. "I'm addicted to you. Your perfect body, the way you taste. The sound of your voice. The way you're my good girl. Everything."

I might have breached her, but she has consumed me.

"Nik," she pants. "I love you."

My heart constricts.

My girl loves me. It tingles down my spine.

Then her words turn into a scream of pleasure, and she pulses around my cock again. She squeezes me and I've never felt anything so good. Watching her come, trembling as she cries out her love for me? The best thing. I'd have that scream as my ringtone if I weren't so insanely possessive of her that the thought of anyone else hearing her come didn't make me murderous.

I grab her hips, lift, and slam her down as I punch upwards, once, twice. And then I'm coming too, like I never have before. Wave after wave as I pull her to me and shake helplessly as I empty into her, roaring her name. Lotte. Rapunzel. Ptichka. In every guise she's mine.

She slumps onto me, and I hold her as close as I can, breathing in her scent, that is home and love.

We lay there, both wrecked by our joining.

It's a long time of whispered names and soft words of love before I have the control over my limbs to carry her to the bath and wash her off.

And when we're back in bed, laid on our sides, I don't want to fall asleep. This moment could last forever, and I'd be happy with it. Content.

"I can still feel the echo of you inside me," she says, exploring my chest with curious fingers. "Like you've changed my body permanently."

"I have." I smooth my hand over her stomach. "You'll be pregnant soon, if you aren't already. You'll be curved and even more gorgeous. I can't wait to see it."

She smiles. "A peace baby."

12

NIKOLAI

One month later

"I have a surprise present for you, husband," Lotte says as we enter the restaurant where we first met, almost exactly a month after our wedding, by my side and holding my hand this time.

"We need to talk about your gifting skills, ptichka," I grumble. Lunch with a man I want to murder but she won't allow me? Not a fantastic gift, let's be honest.

She smothers her laughter and squeezes my fingers. "You'll see."

Hmm. Intriguing.

I do have my suspicions. Lotte was mucking around in the kitchen earlier in a very un-Lotte way.

We've allowed Tottenham to be here waiting, the one graciously welcoming us, as though this was his idea. Lotte requested this meeting, and I'm still not entirely sure why. My sternest enquiries have been met with concrete solid resistance. Apparently, it's better if I don't know.

But whatever my little songbird wants, she gets, so I arranged it.

"Father." She smiles easily, but I notice she doesn't touch him when he rises to greet her. He's not her father, and I wonder if she's going to confront him on that.

"Charlotte." He looks her up and down. "You've put on weight."

"He feeds me well." She hides her smirk as she sits gracefully into the chair opposite her father.

"I love to eat," I comment dryly, seating myself next to my wife.

"Well." Her father snatches up the wine menu and studies it pompously. "Make sure you don't get fat. I won't have you back at Tottenham now you're—"

"Watch your mouth," I snarl, anger rumbling in my chest. "You don't speak to *my wife* like that."

"It's alright, zolotse." Lotte puts her hand on my knee as she calls me *golden one*. She quizzed me a week ago about my name for her, and made me repeat every endearment I could think of until she found something she liked, and has called me that since. I've told her she doesn't need to learn Russian, but that she's making the effort touches my heart.

The waiter is a little more confident than last time we were here. Hopeful that this was the location for the brokering of a peace deal, and reassured that the worst of the risk of blood on the carpet is over.

We order food, and Tottenham requests an outrageously expensive bottle of red wine. Touché. Should have known he'd do that after my little display of wealth over the wedding.

The drinks arrive, and I taste the wine before it's poured for Tottenham and Lotte.

Lotte takes a tiny sip and screws up her face. "Is this corked?"

"No." I'm confused, because Lotte hasn't been drinking recently, and the wine is perfect, if ostentatious.

Tottenham hesitates for a split second, looking at his glass.

"Let me try yours," Lotte says to her father. "Maybe there is something in my glass." She snatches up her father's glass and takes a tiny bit, her face relaxing. "Oh, that's fine."

He grumbles and accepts it back, and as he does, her hand moves oddly.

I attempt to catch her eye, but she steadfastly avoids me. And I wonder…

The starters arrive, and since Lotte didn't tell me not to, I eat oysters with all the echoes of satisfaction from when we first met, and last night when I ate her pussy until she screamed. Got to take what enjoyment I can from this meal.

Lotte daintily eats her salad and pretends not to notice. But I see her cheeks pinkening.

"What did you want to discuss?" Tottenham says around a substantial gulp of wine.

"I have news." She glances over at me, then to her father, eyes bright. "I'm pregnant."

Oh my god. My heart. I'm drowning with pride and happiness.

Pregnant. My wife is pregnant. I'm going to be father to Lotte's child.

Sure, we've been having so much sex it's not a surprise. I've been telling her over and over how I want to breed her. But still, I'm overwhelmed by love for Lotte and the life growing inside her.

A mildly scathing expression crosses Tottenham's face. "Congratulations on your brat."

I growl, but Lotte reaches under the table and pinches my thigh in warning.

"I'm so glad you're pleased you'll be a grandfather." The emphasis makes it sound like she means, *so old you're over the hill and past it*. "And this child started me thinking. They're the future of Tottenham. We should ensure the Tottenham name continues with your Tottenham genetics."

She pulls documents out of her handbag. It was one of the first things she bought when we arrived back in London, and she was enjoying her new life. "This will leave Tottenham to your grandson, when you're gone."

"A new will?" Tottenham gives the papers a dismissive glance.

"Don't you want to ensure your name endures?" Lotte replies. "Everything you've achieved, all the work you put in. It would be a pity for all that to be wasted because you didn't pass it on."

"I don't expect that to be an issue for many years." Tottenham continues eating his beige food.

"Sign it." My voice is granite and iron.

Tottenham looks up, ready for a fight, then stutters as he sees my face.

I don't know why Lotte wants him to sign, but obviously she does. So he will. "Sign it or I'll reverse our peace deal and bankrupt you completely by the time my child is born."

A muscle twitches in Tottenham's jaw, but when Lotte holds out a pen, he snatches it and scrawls his signature onto the page.

"Thank you." Lotte smiles happily. "How is your food? Mine is lovely. I think next time I'll try the oysters. Nik seems to enjoy them so much."

I snort with laughter and Lotte ignores me, chattering on as her father gets visibly annoyed. Red in the face.

Something is up.

"Did you have anything of any actual importance to say?" he snaps eventually, his nose going a deep maroon colour. He blinks and his hand shakes as he takes a long slurp of his wine. Trying to focus on the half-empty glass, he scowls. "You sure this isn't corked? There's a lot of sediment."

"It's not corked," Lotte replies, but her tone has changed completely. Gone is the light and frivolous girlishness.

Tottenham huffs.

"I brought you here because I wanted to talk about my mother and father." Her voice is like I've never heard it. Low, hard, and angry in a totally different way to when she was trying to kill me. There's an undertone of determined fury. Confidence.

"Bad business..." But Tottenham is slurring now.

I look at my wife.

"Are you okay?" she says more loudly and reaches over the table. "What's happening?"

"Nothing," he chokes. "I'm..."

Quick as a flash, she swaps their wine glasses over before taking his hand in hers. And hell, I knew my ptichka was a perfect little potential murderess, but I didn't think she'd be so delightfully sly about it.

Tottenham clutches his chest, going red in the face. He's breathing fast but shallow. A heart attack?

"Go to him," I urge.

Our eyes meet and there's no need for words. We both know what's going on here. I'd have helped if she'd asked, or done it for her. But I almost like it more that she knows she can surprise me, and I won't ask questions. I'll help her clear up any mess. Clever girl though, the evidence will be simple to remove.

"I'm calling an ambulance," I say to the waiter who has just entered. "Get some water."

The waiter flees, happy not to deal with mafia murders, and I flick through my phone to find the number of the doctor I keep on retainer for Edmonton. He answers immediately. A few words and he's on his way.

Lotte is on the other side of the table now, but still, she doesn't touch Tottenham.

"I'll save you, if you tell me the truth," she says, soft but ferocious. "About what happened to my parents. Antonio and my mother."

"Stupid bitch, just get an ambulance," he chokes out. Breathing is difficult for him, and I guess I'm more of a bastard than I thought, because all I care for is Lotte.

"Help! Someone help!" Such an actress.

"The wine..." He gasps as it becomes more impossible for him to breathe.

Lotte's eyebrows pinch together. "But I drank it too?"

David Tottenham slumps.

"No!" she screeches.

The next few minutes are a blur, as a doctor arrives, and we're shooed away. There's an attempt to get his breathing going, and to jump-start his heart.

And when they announce his time of death, it's too much for Lotte. I see the gleam of triumph in her eyes and pull her into my arms, hiding her face against my chest as though she were crying and distraught rather than relieved.

"That was for *your* parents," she whispers. "My gift to you."

My heart constricts. "Thank you."

But not for the gift she thinks she's given me. Yes, it's

nice to have revenge against the man who took my family. But I wanted David Tottenham dead for one thing only: hurting my girl.

And my wife's revenge, the way she wanted it to happen, is the second best present she could give me. The first best?

Our child.

EPILOGUE
NIKOLAI

10 years later

"Who's Daddy's good girl?" I ask, and get a big smile in return. My gaze slides past our youngest daughter and to my wife, who smirks and rolls her eyes from where she's lolling on the sand.

I'm a total sap for my children, but maybe most of all for Svetlana. At only a year old, she's an absolute darling.

Especially when she's not eating sand. I catch Svetlana's hand halfway to her face and wink to Lotte as I mouth, "You're still my best girl."

Lotte's smile turns smug. She knows I adore her. I show her just how much every night and far too many mornings for a busy family.

"Why can't I be a good girl?" grumbles Ivan, our eldest boy from where he's patting sand into a bucket for another part of his sandcastle.

"You can be a good girl. Or a good boy," Lotte replies. "If you don't tease the waiter at the restaurant tonight."

We're going to our restaurant this evening, for our anniversary.

"Or a bad boy," I add, and Ivan's eyes light up. "The waiter was fine. I wasn't going to do anything. It was just a joke."

Lotte rolls her eyes. "Then you need to be clearer with them, zolotse. Poor guy nearly had a heart attack last time Ivan said he'd get his dad to kill him because they didn't have any salted caramel ice cream."

"Noted. No death threats over ice cream, Ivan. Needs to be at least a whole course before we threaten even maiming. Got it?"

"'Spose so." Ivan is intent on his castle, which is good, because Lotte is half laughing, half exasperated with my joke as she closes her eyes.

I scoop up a spade and offer it to our youngest daughter. "No more sand though, as you've got a delicious restaurant dinner coming up this evening."

The restaurant, deep into Lambeth territory, was surprised when we rebooked to eat there a month after Lotte's father died. They understandably imagined this place would have negative connotations, aside from being in a rival part of London. But no. There are only good memories, and the London Mafia Syndicate has reduced the animosity between those who have joined.

It's sentimental, but I like to spend our wedding anniversary eating at the restaurant where we first met. When Ivan was only six months old, we went there for our second wedding anniversary and caused many hidden English looks of surprise at us bringing a baby into an exclusive and outrageously expensive restaurant. They're used to us now, but that first time I think a waiter had to go out and buy a highchair. It still had a tag on it when it was presented, and sweat was wiped from the waiter's brow as he walked away.

The Tottenham-Edmonton feud might be over, but our new combined mafia is one that Londoners are wary of.

I am still notoriously murderous. There aren't many London mafia bosses who have killed as many of the people related to them as I have. The rumours about our involvement in Lotte's father's death are firmly denied and silenced.

It won't do for her music career to have any hint of her true, beautiful, ruthless self in her image of innocence and empowerment. Obviously, she doesn't need the money, but she loves to sing, and even though she's busy as a mother and co-leader of the Edmonton and Tottenham mafia, she always finds time to post a video.

Sometimes from this beach, or others, but just as often singing in that sound booth I made for her in our Edmonton house. She can use it on her own now. For many years it induced panic attacks unless I was with her. Never a chore, because I love listening to her sing, but I was proud as fuck when the video she made pinged onto my phone, and I realised what she'd been brave enough to do. In the end, we pushed back all the darkness her father tried to put on her.

Ivan sits back and regards his finished castle.

"Can we make it go boom like the tower?" he asks Lotte.

She laughs. "You've got a taste for blowing things up now, have you?"

"Yep." Ivan stands and looks with pride at his sandcastle. "This one isn't good. We'll make another one better."

My throat clogs, because he's echoing what Lotte said when Tottenham Tower came down.

It's ironic that the reason we ended up together was my uncle trying to blow up Tottenham Tower, since Lotte did almost exactly that last year. Turns out it was structurally unstable. Her father had built an extra penthouse floor which wasn't accounted for in the original design, and the whole thing was about to collapse under the weight of his own greed and folly.

If that's not a metaphor, I don't know what is.

"Will you help, Mummy?"

Lotte is on her feet in a second, at Ivan's side. "You know I'm always up for some tower demolition."

I pull Svetlana into my lap for safety and watch with amusement as Lotte and Ivan trample the castle with gleeful comments about how it is falling down excellently, and they can't wait to build another.

"We're going to have to buy them Jenga to satisfy their building and destructive impulses," I mutter to Svetlana.

"Well, that worked up an appetite," Lotte says, dusting off her hands as though a good day's work has been achieved. "How about dinner at our favourite restaurant?"

Ivan perks up, then furrows his brow. "Can we come back here though? I want to build another castle."

"Definitely," I say. "You'll be here tomorrow, because we'll return tonight."

I catch Lotte's hand in mine and kiss her knuckles. That spark is in her brown eyes again. The one that says, *I love you and I'm going to surprise you.*

I wink.

It's indulgent, but we always come home to the beach house after our anniversary dinner. For no better reason than because this is where I should have taken her that first night. Sentimental, like I said. The kids get tucked into bed, usually having been asleep already—somehow. Lotte put in a large flat lawn at the side of the house as a helicopter pad, so now we don't even have to drive the last part of the journey.

Maybe I'll take her down to the beach. My little songbird always deserves a treat.

EXTENDED EPILOGUE
LOTTE

10 years later, that night

It's dark and the moon is up as we walk down the steps to the beach. The moon is full, and the night still. When my feet touch the sand, it's soft and gritty and slightly warm from the heat of the day.

Nik is at my back, and smooths his hands over my shoulders.

"I'm hungry, ptichka..." he growls. And I know he doesn't mean food, not just because we ate a delicious dinner only a few hours ago, but because he adds, "You're my favourite dessert..."

Much as I long to lean back into his embrace and let him love me sweet and slow, I have planned for this. It's something I've been wanting to do for a while, and we've talked about. I step forward and turn, then walk backwards as he narrows his eyes and stalks towards me. He toes off his shoes and socks and continues to advance on me.

Such a stalker, my husband.

My pussy heats at the dark look on his face. He's intent,

silver eyes glittering and my breath catches. He's wearing a custom made black tuxedo, but removed the bow tie and unbuttoned the shirt up at the house. There's a bulge at the front of his trousers, as well as a smaller one to the side. A baby monitor, for him to ensure his little ones are safe, even as we indulge.

He's such a good dad. It's hot af.

"I'm not your meal, zolotse. This bird won't be caught and eaten by the lion so easily," I tease.

He smiles, wide and feral. "Oh won't she? Go on then. Try. Fly."

Spinning on my heel, I dash away, holding my skirt up away from my legs.

"If I catch you, I'm going to feast on you, little bird," he shouts after me.

I laugh with delight at the freedom of this. To run. Play. Fight, even.

It's just seconds before I hear him coming after me, heavy footsteps.

I make right for the sea before veering to the right to sprint along the slushy water where the waves meet the sand, spray kicking up with my heels.

My heart beats hard, and I'm thruming with adrenaline. Excitement. Love. Lust. It's a heady cocktail that is familiar and wonderful everytime we do this. The night is dark and warm, the scent of the sea in my nostrils. My legs burn with the effort, and I pump my arms.

"I'm coming for you," Nik growls, right behind me.

I shriek and put on a burst of speed, and I'm torn between desperately wanting to be caught, and the primal urge to escape a scary predator.

I manage six more steps before Nik wraps his arms around my waist and tumbles us to the ground, twisting in the air so he takes the brunt of the force and I land on top. I snatch up my dress and pull the ornamental dagger from its holster on my thigh, whipping it to his throat. I put on the softest pressure. Not enough to break the skin.

Straddling him, I get his thick cock that I like so much, that has brought me pleasure after pleasure on many nights where I've screamed his name, hoarse after coming so many times I gave up counting, right at my entrance through his clothes. I'm not wearing any knickers, in anticipation of this moment. We both groan, and I love that. My desperate husband, still always wanting to be inside me even as I threaten him with a knife.

I love him so much.

I'm soaking wet, and he's hard and I need him. Being with Nik is intoxicating.

"You're a bad, bad man, husband," I purr, and slide the blade over his skin.

"My bloodthirsty ptichka," he murmurs and stretches out his neck, a calculating smile on his face. "Don't bite the man who fucks you."

Unbuttoning his trousers lazily, he shoves them and his boxers down, ignoring the knife and the fact I'm on top of him, focused on getting us skin to skin.

"Better give me an orgasm so I forget what I was annoyed with you about."

"I will." He brings his hand to my neck and grips the back with his fingers, running his thumb over my windpipe. "So vibrant," he whispers. "So alive. I can feel your pulse. It's fast. Do you like this?"

He rolls his hips and his hardness sinks into where I'm wet and ready for him, just the tip.

"And wet too. You're life, ptichka. Everything to me."

He pushes further as I hold the knife to his throat, and

he has his thumb partially restricting the very air I breathe. It's the ultimate in trust and unspeakably heady. I could take his life, he could take mine.

"My love." I sink down further.

He stretches me and there's a pinch of hurt. He is so big that every time it's an invasion. Then my pussy gives. That moment when he's inside me right to the hilt is mind-stealing. My hand drops away, knife falling.

"My *wife.*"

He lets go of my neck and rolls me under him, bracing himself on one forearm as he simultaneously reaches between us and finds my clit, and pounds into me.

Thrust after thrust of his body into mine until we're both panting and I can't tell whose voice is whining—probably me—and grunting—probably Nik.

There's no thought of escape now, only pleasure crashing into me, harder and higher with every time he shoves his cock right where I need it. In me, all the way. Filling me.

I surrender to him and to the orgasm that hits me in waves.

There's nothing but endless pleasure, barbed and sweet and sparkling.

I only realise I've closed my eyes when it's sounds that bring me back.

The sea. The waves are shushing us as Nik tells me in a gravelly voice that I'm his good girl. That he loves me, and feeling me come around his cock is the best part of his life. That he's going to fill me up with another baby.

A tug to my hair and I open my eyes. He's there. Then he shifts, pulling out of me and I cry out at the loss, my pussy fluttering at the emptiness.

"Don't worry, ptichka, I'm going to take care of you."

While I'm still boneless and riding the aftershocks of coming, he grabs my arse and leans over me, bringing my wet, open slit to his mouth. Then he licks. A long, slow stroke from my entrance right over my clit. Again. Then again. Giving me a little time to adjust before he shortens the licks more and more, faster and right over my clit.

He devours me. He sucks and bites and drags out my previous orgasm into something new and almost painful it's so good.

I'm writhing and sobbing, overcome, so aroused, impossibly on the point of coming a second time when just as abruptly as he began, he dumps me back onto the wet sand and covers me with his body.

My husband's patience has run out.

He rams into my pussy, uncompromising, and the contrast to his sucking my clit pulls a whine from my chest, almost tipping me into orgasm.

I look up, wanting to remember this as clearly as I do so many special nights together.

This man is everything. My whole world in his shadowed face. In the moonlight his grey eyes are black with dark desire and his expression is full of awe and fierce concentration as, keeping one hand in my hair, he runs the other lazily to my neck, cupping it. He holds my throat in a gentle but firm clasp, his thumb over my windpipe and his fingertips pressing into my nape. His thumb is insistent but controlled.

My clit throbs from his thumb putting just enough pressure on my windpipe. That one touch shoots right down my body in a flood of pleasure. It's no more than a caress as he keeps fucking into me, but it's enough to give me sensation that shines as bright as the moon above us.

He's getting harder and bigger, swelling in my pussy

and we look into each other's eyes. There's no pain, he's not cutting off any air supply.

But he *could*.

It's pure dominance. His hand around my neck is a statement of ownership. It says, my life is in his hands, and I trust him with that. I'm happy to give over everything to him, and he'll take it.

"Come for me again, Lotte," he demands and instantly that hand that was at my throat is at my clit again, circling the little bud remorselessly, shifting to shallow thrusts that he knows drive me out of my mind because the thick head of his cock hits that place near my entrance that seems to be connected to my clit. My body throbs in time to his thrusts.

There's no saying no to this man, as if I ever would. There's only, "Yes."

I grip his hips and dig my heels into his buttocks, urging him on, pulling him deeper as I know he needs.

He moans, and it's the sweetest sound in the world.

My husband unravels as I come again. I shake with the pleasure coursing through me and he's an earthquake over and inside me. And this time I don't close my eyes and neither does he. As he fills me to the brim with wet heat, he roars my name and stares into my eyes, that absolute focus on my face makes the clenches of my orgasm reach up to my heart.

My husband loves me as much as I love him. Maybe even more.

It's minutes before we both are motionless and drained. Satisfied.

He clasps my face in his palms, strokes his thumbs over my cheeks and then leans in for a lingering kiss that's loving and delicate after the frenetic power of our sex.

It's always like this with Nik. He is strong and overpowering, and it's important to remind him of my power too. Hence the knife.

But he's also adoring and protective.

Dawn is breaking by the time we walk back up the steps to the house, salty from a swim. We're arm in arm as we walk into the house, so content. The children have slept like angels and we've made love and fucked and got sand in places sand shouldn't be all night.

I'm sore, and I think I might have bruises. Today might be a long day without any sleep. But Nik will take the kids if I need a nap, and then I can return the favour.

And I know tonight we'll have a repeat. Whether in our own bed with soft sheets or on the beach with animalistic vibes, it's always the two of us. Together.

THANKS

Thank you for reading, I hope you enjoyed it.

Want to read a little more Happily Ever After? Click to get exclusive epilogues and free stories! or head to EvieRoseAuthor.com

If you have a moment, I'd really appreciate a review wherever you like to talk about books. Reviews, however brief, help readers find stories they'll love.

Love to get the news first? Follow me on your favored social media platform - I love to chat to readers and you get all the latest gossip.

If the newsletter is too much like commitment, I recommend following me on BookBub, where you'll just get new release notifications and deals.

- amazon.com/author/evierose
- bookbub.com/authors/evie-rose
- instagram.com/evieroseauthor
- tiktok.com/@EvieRoseAuthor

INSTALOVE BY EVIE ROSE

Grumpy Bosses

Older Hotter Grumpier

My billionaire boss catches my reading when I should be working. And the punishment…?

London Mafia Bosses

Captured by the Mafia Boss

I might be an innocent runaway, but I'm at my friend's funeral to avenge her murder by the mafia boss: King.

Taken by the Kingpin

Tall, dark, older and dangerous, I shouldn't want him.

I thought my mafia connections were in the past, and I was alone. But powerful mafia boss Sebastian Laurent hasn't forgotten me.

Stolen by the Mafia King

I didn't know he has been watching me all this time.

I had a plan to escape. Everything is going perfectly at my wedding rehearsal dinner until *he* turns up.

Caught by the Kingpin

The kingpin growls a warning that I shouldn't try his patience by attempting to escape.

There's no way I'm staying as his little prisoner.

Claimed by the Mobster

I'm in love with my ex-boyfriend's dad: a dangerous and powerful mafia boss twice my age.

Snatched by the Bratva

I have an excruciating crush on this man who comes into the coffee shop. Every day. He's older, gorgeous, perfectly dressed. He has a Russian accent and silver eyes.

Filthy Scottish Kingpins

Forbidden Appeal

He's older and rich, and my teenage crush re-surfaces as I beg the former kingpin to help me escape a mafia arranged marriage. He stares at me like I'm a temptress he wants to banish, but we're snowed in at his Scottish castle.

Captive Desires

I was sent to kill him, but he's captured me, and I'm at his mercy. He says he'll let me go if I beg him to take his...

Mafia Boss Marriage

Owned by her Enemy

I didn't expect the ruthless new kingpin—an older man, gorgeous and hard—to extract such a price for a ceasefire: a mafia arranged marriage.

Marrying the Boss

Baby Proposal

My boss walked in on me buying "magic juice" online... And now he's demanding to be my baby's daddy!

Printed in Dunstable, United Kingdom